Friendship inspired this story and friends helped every step of the way. I am delighted to say that working with 918studio press opened up new friendships. I want to thank Jodie Toohey for her deft editorial touch and Lori Perkins for her mastery of printing and publication.

A decade and a half of participation in the Thursday Morning Writing Group in Madison, Wisconsin, has forged many friendships. The critiques and encouragement received from group members have improved every story I have shared with them. I am particularly beholden to Zach Elliot, Ingrid Kallick, Gypsy Thomas, and Sarah Moser for the time and intelligence they gave to critiquing *Another Life*. Sue Brewster and Kate McKinney are new faces who have provided the type of boost that helps morale during the process of seeking publication. Ingrid Kallick, of course, deserves a second mention for her beautiful cover art.

Misty Urban and Kathleen Ernst, exceptional writers and good friends, were kind enough to read *Another Life* and offer comments. Support and assistance from Debbie Kmetz has been vital to my writing for almost two decades. Writers always rely on family as well as friends for support. I thank my wife, Joyce, for her patience with the time and resources I devote to writing stories.

Ultimately, stories are meant for readers. I am exceptionally fortunate to have two special readers. Susan Collins has an uncanny ability to express insights into my work that I am not always able to articulate on my own. Pam Durian graciously gives of her time to read stories I have completed. Her generous friendship helped me to believe that *Another Life* is worth sharing.

PROLOGUE

How many fantasies come true? Not passing little daydreams. Big, ridiculous, life-changing fantasies. Somehow, the fantasy wedding was going to happen.

Funny how Matt Cooper had almost forgotten about it after so many years. Of course, how many teenage boys fantasize about weddings? Back then, Matt knew that was different, but he had spent most of his teenage years feeling different. What the heck. People are who they are. For a while, Matt blamed not fitting in on his father. His dad sold the drugstore in Garwin, took a job at a big pharmacy in Des Moines, and moved the family to Ankeny when Matt was fourteen. Freshmen in high school go where their parents take them. So while all of Matt's classmates appeared to be making seamless transitions from the junior high two blocks down the street, he was the new kid from a little town that the other teenagers in Ankeny had probably never heard of.

Meeting Kimberly Gustafson only made Matt more

aware of being out of place. It didn't seem possible that any girl could be so pretty. He didn't have a word for the ache she put inside him. Matt already felt like he didn't measure up to a class full of kids who all knew what to wear, what to say, how to stand, when to laugh, and every other detail of how to navigate Ankeny High. But Kimberly Gustafson? She represented a whole different universe of not measuring up. Even when he stood behind her in the cafeteria line, Matt felt he would never really be any closer than admiring her from afar.

Then Kim surprised him. In addition to being a cheerleader, homecoming queen, student council president, and cute beyond his dreams, she turned out to be nice. She said, "Hi," to him in the college prep classes they had together, smiled at him when they passed in the halls, and asked him to buy candy from her for the drama club fundraiser. To Matt, she remained the incomparable, unattainable, naturally blond beauty, but at least, she was a nice incomparable, unattainable, naturally blond beauty. And then, only thirty-eight years later, the fantasy came true.

CHAPTER ONE

Matt pushed back from the round oak table loaded with food and patted his stomach. It was such a cliché, but what else could you do after one of Carol's Thanksgiving dinners? They had been married for thirty-two years, and each Thanksgiving feast seemed even a little bit better than the one before. This year, Carol added a homemade orange-cranberry relish from heaven. He could tell by the comments around the table that the relish would become a Cooper family tradition, taking a regular place alongside the candied yams, French-style green beans, Parmesan-crusted dinner rolls, mashed potatoes and giblet gravy, rutabagas, pickled beets, sage dressing, and roast turkey slowly basted by the fat from strips of thick, smoky bacon perched on top. Matt raided the turkey platter one more time and popped a crisp crumb of bacon into his mouth. He didn't need one more bite, but he knew everyone else at the table was also so stuffed that dessert would wait until later. The pumpkin and mincemeat pies had safe homes on wire racks in the kitchen. Carol always made mincemeat even though Matt was the only one of the four of them who liked it.

The living room couch beckoned as the perfect place to fall asleep in front of a football game. Eric would probably stay awake and actually watch. That would be good since Eric could update him when Matt regained consciousness from his turkey-induced stupor. Angie would likely take a straightforward nap in her room after her late night flight in from San Francisco. The change in Denver, ride home from Des Moines, and larger demands presented by graduate school had to be adding up by now. Of course, Matt would offer to help Carol clear. Tradition would hold there, too, when she told him that the last thing she needed was him putting things where it would take her the rest of next week to find them. Who didn't love tradition?

"Great meal, Mom," Eric said. He spoke again before Matt and Angie could add their congratulations. "I've got something to tell everybody."

For an instant, Matt's mind flashed to his job at the college and to Edwin, his best friend there. Edwin loved to tell the story of how he announced to his family at the end of a Thanksgiving dinner that he was gay. As Matt's kids moved into, and in Eric's case, through their mid-twenties unmarried, Edwin enjoyed teasing that Matt's turn for a holiday surprise was coming.

"You know I've been seeing somebody," Eric said.

"Know wouldn't exactly be the word," Carol answered. "Guessed. Hoped."

"Prayed." Angie giggled.

"You don't keep us very well informed on that score," Matt said.

"I've mentioned Julie."

"You've mentioned some Julie that you work with," Carol said.

Eric folded his napkin and placed it on the table. "I do work with her . . . sort of."

"Sort of?" his mom asked.

"She does basketball games. I've been seeing her. I guess you could say you've all been seeing her. You, anyway, Dad. She's on TV."

Matt had coached basketball at the college for almost thirty years. When Eric starred as a swimmer in high school and then entered college with the goal of pursuing an MBA, it seemed that his life would end up as far away from college basketball as possible. Then came a good job offer from the NCAA in Indianapolis, and soon Eric was a media liaison for the national basketball tournament. Not the national tournament for small colleges like Matt coached, but the big one. March Madness. Suddenly it clicked.

"You don't mean Julie Johnson?" Matt said.

"Actually, I do. We've been going out."

"Who's Julie Johnson?" Carol asked.

Carol knew as much about sports as Matt did about cleaning up after Thanksgiving dinner.

"She's a sideline reporter," Matt said. "She does network games all the time, and of course, the tournament. She's on . . . she's uh . . ."

"What, Dad?" Angie asked. "Hot?"

"I was going to say famous. She's on TV all the time.

Eric, I mean wow." Matt patted the table.

"It's not that big of a deal," Eric said. "The tournament's my job. You didn't think I'd meet the announcers?"

"I know that, but she's . . ."

"Hot?" Angie chimed in again.

"She's a very pretty young woman," Matt said to Angie.

"I think so," Eric said, "but she likes to be thought of as more than pretty."

"She does a great job, Eric. You can tell she knows her basketball."

"Glad you approve. People like to make a good impression on their future in-laws."

"What?"

"Julie and I are engaged."

"Eric!" Carol clapped her hand over her mouth and knocked over her empty wine glass in the process. Matt grabbed it by the stem just as it rolled over the edge of the table. He could see the relieved look in Angie's eyes. A prospective marriage would have been off to a bad start if one of Carol's favorite crystal wine glasses had been sacrificed to the shock of the announcement.

"Engaged," Matt said. "That's great. Congratulations, Eric!"

"Isn't it kind of fast?" Angie asked.

"We've been dating for a while," Eric said. "She's a year younger than me. I guess we're getting to an age where we're both ready. We didn't want to wait."

Matt wondered how long Eric meant by "a while." He had mentioned going out with somebody in a couple of his weekly phone calls, but Matt and Carol had no idea it was anything serious. Certainly not anything with a famous woman who looked like a movie star.

"Honey, I wish you would have told us something sooner." Carol's words picked up Matt's unspoken thoughts in the uncanny way of a couple married for thirty-two years.

"There wasn't anything to tell until last week. It's not like the wedding is tomorrow. We're thinking next summer."

"But we had no idea there was somebody this special in your life," Carol said. "It seems like something you would share with your parents."

Matt wondered if Carol really believed that. Eric had always guarded his dating like some kind of national secret. That made some sense. Carol lived for her children and had always loved being involved in their lives. She never actually interfered in their dating, but that possibility must have crossed both Eric's and Angie's minds as they grew up. It didn't seem to bother Angie as much. At least, she was never as guarded. Probably some woman-to-woman thing between Carol and their daughter that Matt would never understand.

"Summer weddings are lovely," Carol said. "There's so much that you can do. I always love catering weddings in a garden. The tents, the flowers, the streamers. It can all be so beautiful."

"You're getting a little ahead of yourself," Eric said. "We haven't talked about any plans at all."

"Oh, honey, I wasn't implying I'd cater, but come to think of it, I should know the date as soon as you decide. It would be a disaster if I scheduled to cater a wedding on the day you get married. In twenty years, I've never had to pull out on anybody."

"I hadn't thought about your business," Eric said. "We can try to set a date ASAP. I'm sure Julie will understand."

"And your sister will have to make travel plans from the West Coast," Carol said. "I suppose Indianapolis is easy to get to."

"The wedding will be in Iowa. Julie's from Cedar Rapids," Eric said. "Dad, you might even know her mother."

"I don't remember any Johnsons from Cedar Rapids."

"Her mom went to Ankeny High School. Her maiden name was Gustafson."

Suddenly, the name Johnson did ring a bell. Matt hadn't seen Kim since graduation, but he remembered somebody telling him that she married a dentist from Marion. That guy's name was Johnson. Anybody who had ever been to Marion knew that it ran right together with Cedar Rapids. A successful dentist from Marion would be a prime candidate to live in one of the nicer neighborhoods in Cedar Rapids.

"Earth to Dad," Eric said. "Did you know her? Kim Gustafson?"

"We had some classes together. Kim was one of the popular kids. You know, cheerleader. Different group than I ran in."

"That's unbelievable," Angie said. She touched her dad's arm. "Probably an old flame."

"Just somebody I went to school with. Definitely out of my league. I mean, I knew she married some guy named Johnson, but I had no idea about this Julie

Johnson."

"This Julie Johnson?" Eric said. "Sounds kind of impersonal for my fiancée."

"Johnson's a common name is all. I mean Julie Johnson could be a stage name."

"Stage name?" Angie giggled.

"Well, she is in television. People use names for TV. The first and last both start with the same letter. You know, it's . . . it's . . . what do you call it?"

"Alliteration, dear," Carol said.

"Yeah, that's it. Alliteration. That could be a stage name."

"Well, it's not," Eric said. "Trust me. It's her real name, and you get to meet the real person at Christmas."

"That will be lovely, honey," Carol said, "but don't forget about the wedding date. It really would help me if you can decide before Christmas."

The words "wedding date" echoed in Matt's head. This was the wedding he had fantasized about all those years ago in high school. Though he knew he could never approach Kim Gustafson's universe, more than one night he lay in bed thinking someday he could have a son and Kim could have a daughter. Their kids would be the ones to marry. He didn't know why, but the idea seemed romantic to him, like a fairy tale. Now, in Indianapolis, Indiana, of all places, the fairy tale had come true. His ridiculous fantasy would become a reality. Matt looked at his empty wine glass and wished he had a good long swallow left.

CHAPTER TWO

"So, how well did you know Julie's mother?"

Carol's question, tossed over her shoulder as she walked from the bedroom into the bath, came without a hint of jealousy.

"Just like I said at dinner. We had a lot of the same classes, but she was in that elite group. You know how high school is."

"Was, dear. We're at the age when the past tense is very much in order with regard to high school."

The sounds of a faucet turning on and Carol brushing her teeth confirmed a reading of zero on the potential jealousy meter. Matt didn't know why that should bother him. Kim wasn't anybody he ever talked about. He couldn't remember her entering his mind in years. Well, nothing more than briefly, anyway. He probably had never said her name to Carol. Still, a touch of jealousy from his wife might have been nice.

Carol loved him. He never questioned that, but he knew she loved him first as the father of her children and second as her husband. Carol might say there was no difference, but Matt could always feel it. She threw herself into home and children with a passion that filled her life. Luckily for Eric and Angie, Carol had discovered catering as a way to siphon off some of her rampaging domesticity. The time she devoted to her business actually provided the kids with a reasonable buffer against smothering mothering.

Matt and Carol met in college. Her English major remained in their lives as a vestige popping up when she provided him a word like alliteration or suggested what tense he should use when speaking about high school. Her career as a high school English teacher lasted only two years. Eric came along, and that's when home and family became the focus of Carol's being.

Matt didn't complain. Her absolute devotion to the home fires allowed him the freedom to give as much time as he wanted to the career he fell into the same year that Eric was born. Matt used his history major even less than Carol employed her English degree. His move to Ankeny at the age of fourteen had resulted in the starting eighth-grade point guard from Garwin not even being good enough to sit on the end of the bench for the Ankeny High basketball team. Attending a small college brought yet another change in his basketball fortunes. This time, he made the team—and was just barely good enough to sit on the end of the bench. He rode the pines for four years.

Four years on the team sitting, watching, and

listening to the coach proved to be a pretty good apprenticeship. After graduation, Coach Anderson offered him a quarter-time position as his assistant and hooked him up with a second part-time job in the admissions department. Matt served as one of the freshly-minted graduates that small colleges loved to have showing pimply-faced prospective students around campus.

The next year, Coach Anderson suffered a stroke in midseason. Suddenly, Matt became the interim coach. The college asked Matt to stay the following season and hold the position until Coach Anderson recovered. What came seven months later was not recovery, but a fatal heart attack. At age twenty-four, the college took the word interim off of Matt's title, and he had been the head coach ever since.

He turned out to be good at coaching and clever enough to realize the charms of doing it at a small college. Winning an occasional conference championship and showing up at events when the president asked him proved to be more than adequate performance to hold the position for three decades. No one at the local high school looked askance at Eric turning out to be a swimmer instead of a star basketball player as might have been expected of a major college coach's son. Certainly, small college basketball didn't require Matt to spend half of his life trying to attract eighteen-year-olds with enormous basketball talent, and even bigger egos, to campus. Those players went to the Big Ten, the Big Twelve, or the Big Someplace—not to the Iowa Conference.

Not that Matt's job didn't require time. Every away

game meant hours driving the team van. Many other nights Matt spent in some high school gym letting a decent player (with the grades good enough to get into a good liberal arts college) know that his talents were appreciated. Making an appearance at a kid's game was the biggest recruiting tool for a college with no athletic scholarships.

Carol never complained about all of the winter nights when Matt didn't arrive home until midnight or later. When the college filled out his appointment by making Matt director of intramural sports, Carol happily supported his need to be on campus presenting a ping pong trophy or filling in as a last-minute umpire for a coed kickball game. Nothing pleased her more than having the total responsibility for getting dinner on the table for Eric and Angie, making sure they brushed their teeth, or helping them with their homework. The fact that both were excellent students probably made the latter responsibility easier, but Carol's guidance no doubt had a lot to do with the kids' success.

"Did you hear what I said?"

Matt hadn't heard, or if he did, it didn't register.

"I'm done in the bathroom," Carol said.

"Oh, sorry. Thanks."

"Your mind is someplace else tonight."

"I think maybe I overdosed on Thanksgiving dinner. That second piece of mincemeat pie might have done it. I think it was your best ever."

"Why thank you, dear." Carol bent down and kissed him on the cheek. "Do you have enough energy to get up from the edge of the bed and make your way into the bathroom?"

"You could help," he said.

She leaned in and slid her arms under his. He liked the feel of her satin nightgown against his face as she playfully tugged him up to a standing position. When he got to his feet, he kissed the top of her head.

"It's wonderful about Eric," Carol said.

"That it is, though you'd think he might have given us some small indication before."

"Even so, I'm so happy for him. What about this girl's mother?"

"What about what?" Matt said, letting go of his embrace around Carol.

"You made it sound like she was standoffish. Cheerleader. Elite group. I hope she wasn't one of those nasty 'in' girls that always ran around together in high school."

"She was perfectly nice. I just didn't fit in that well. I've told you how it was for me, moving from Garwin."

"Tonight, I'm not as concerned about your teenage trials, dear, as I am about Eric's future mother-in-law."

"And I repeat, she was perfectly nice." Matt stepped into the bathroom and picked up the tube of toothpaste that Carol always kept expertly rolled up from the bottom.

"Are you looking forward to seeing her again?" Carol asked from the bedroom.

"I suppose. Though, if you think about it, I've never been to a high school reunion. I guess I can't claim to be super interested."

"I would think it would be nice for you to see her," Carol said.

"Nicer to meet Eric's fiancée," Matt answered.

"Anyway, I have to brush my teeth." He stuck the toothbrush in his mouth before any more lies came out.

CHAPTER THREE

"Is that our exit?" Carol pointed through the windshield toward a large green highway sign.

"That's the one," Matt answered. He patted her knee.

"I guess that means we're almost there."

"It's not too far from the interstate," Matt said as he drove down the exit ramp. "Almost there" was the nicest thing Carol had said since they left home an hour and twenty minutes ago.

"I still don't see the point of going to the Amanas."

"It's neutral ground," Matt said. "Eric and Julie wanted her folks and us to meet. They picked out a restaurant in between our place and theirs."

"Well, the Amana Colonies are definitely closer to them," she said as he made his turn onto a county blacktop.

"A little." Matt sped up. "They have good food."

"Matt, I could have fixed a lovely meal."

"Of course you could have, dear. Maybe this is just symbolism. The Amanas serve family-style. We're all going to be family."

"I don't think there's anything more family-style than eating at a family table."

Matt didn't answer. Trotting out the word *symbolism* hadn't swayed Carol, despite her English major roots.

"I just wish I understood," she said. "I would have been very willing to have everybody at our house. Eric knows that."

"Kim and Wayne have a house, too."

"I think that's obvious, Matt." Carol looked away.

"My sense is that Wayne is very into showing off their house. I think that was the problem. Wayne is apparently pretty house-centric, and you are perhaps a little hospitality-centric."

She turned back to face him. "Oh, for heaven's sake, Matt, what does hospitality-centric mean?"

"You love to entertain."

"And what's wrong with that?"

"Nothing, but you're sort of . . . uh . . . uh . . . a force of nature."

"You want to try that in plain English, dear?"

"You know," Matt said. "That movie we like, *Forces of Nature*. The woman is totally . . . uh totally . . . you know, Sandra Bullock's role."

"I'm like Sandra Bullock!"

"You think Sandra Bullock is good."

"Sandra Bullock was a borderline lunatic in that movie."

"She's pretty. You look like Sandra Bullock."

"Phht." Carol rolled her eyes. "If I was twenty years younger."

"Point well taken, dear. That means that technically she looks like you."

"Nice try. I wonder if she's hospitality-centric, too."

"That was a bad choice of words," Matt said. "I needed an editor—"

"Or a muzzle." Carol turned a little more toward him. "Do you really think I look like Sandra Bullock?"

"As a matter of fact, I do." Matt wondered why he hadn't ever noticed it before. Sandra Bullock was one of his favorites. Maybe her resemblance to a younger Carol was one of the reasons why.

"So Eric says Julie's father is house-centric?" Carol asked.

"Something like that. Not exactly those words. They apparently have a pretty nice place."

"You mean he likes to show off his money."

"Eric didn't put it that way." Matt saw a sign that read: Middle Amana – Five Miles. Those five miles couldn't pass fast enough.

"You wouldn't think a dentist would be that rich," Carol said.

"He's an orthodontist."

Carol nodded. It didn't seem to Matt that being an orthodontist actually should be an automatic reason for someone being rich, but it clearly satisfied Carol. She probably couldn't conceive of parents who weren't willing to pay whatever the price to give their children straight teeth. He found it endearing in its own way. It was so Carol.

"I hope that's not a problem for Eric," she said.

"What's not a problem?"

"Having rich in-laws."

"Rich might be overstating it, dear. I'm guessing Wayne does well for a dentist, but it's not like Eric has a bad job. And Julie has to make plenty working on national TV."

"Which will make Eric low man on the financial totem pole all the way around."

"You're worrying way too much about money. Eric is fine."

"It isn't just money. Here we are meeting at some restaurant. And they're going to Julie's home for Christmas. It's just one thing after another."

"They're coming to our house for Christmas Eve."

"That's not the same thing," Carol said.

"It's when we do our presents."

"That tradition's from your side of the family, Matt."

"Carol, we've been married for thirty-two years. It seems like by now it would be our family tradition."

"It's just not the same." Carol stared out the passenger side window into the darkness. "I can't even think of the dinner table on Christmas Day. Just you and I and Angie. It will be the first time Eric isn't there."

"I guess you could look at it this way—"

"Oh never mind, Matt. I don't want to talk about it. Not now."

In Matt's marriage, *I don't want to talk about it* were big words. Way too big to fit comfortably in their minivan. Carol always wanted to talk things through. Almost always. The last time she didn't want to talk about something, Matt had put a walnut shell down her garbage disposal, tried to free the resulting jam with a fork, blown a fuse for the main kitchen circuit, shut down her catering oven, and caused four cheesecakes to fall. It happened five years ago, but the pain of *I don't want to talk about it* came back to him as clearly as banging his head on the gutters yesterday while putting up Christmas decorations. Luckily, escape from the minivan loomed ahead in the form of a rambling building in the simple style of the Amana Colonies. He and Carol had eaten at the restaurant several times and always liked it. It felt like tonight definitely would be the exception.

"Here we are," he said.

"I know, dear."

As they walked toward the restaurant, Matt instinctively looked for Eric's car in the parking lot before he cleared away the haze of Carol's snit enough to remember that Eric and Julie had flown in special for the occasion. They would have driven a rental from the airport. Or maybe Julie's parents drove them. For the sake of this meal, he hoped that wasn't the case. Carol was upset enough already. He opened the door and saw Eric waiting for them near the hostess station.

"Mom, Dad, you're right on time." Eric hugged his mother and then shook Matt's hand.

"Sweetie, what a treat to see you again so soon. I'll have to thank Julie for that." Carol hugged him again. "Where is she?"

"She's already at the table with her folks. They picked us up at the airport."

"How nice of them." Carol's jaw tightened.

"It made the most sense for us to fly into Cedar Rapids. It was right on their way to drive us here."

"Oh, do they live near the airport?" Carol asked.

"No, but they had to go right by," Eric answered.

"I'm sure it was the practical thing to do," Carol said. "Either way, it's good to have you home, or at least this close to home."

"Well, let's not stand here waiting," Matt said. He put his arm around Carol's waist and edged her toward the dining room. "I'm anxious to meet everybody."

"Pardon me for enjoying a moment with our son." Carol stiffened, but turned and walked at Matt's side. She didn't seem to be enjoying anything.

They entered the large open dining area, and Matt immediately recognized Julie Johnson sitting at a round table beside a bow window curtained in blue gingham. She looked even more beautiful in person than on TV. Beside her sat a bald, barrel-chested man and a trim woman in a green cable knit sweater. Matt knew two things immediately. Kim had married a football player, and Matt would not have recognized her if they had passed on the street. Age had darkened her silky blond hair, and the straight, shiny locks that hung to her shoulders as a teenager had become the short, wavy hairdo of a woman in her mid-fifties. While the Cooper family approached the table, the Johnson family rose as one. In that moment, the warm, simple smile that had pierced Matt's heart in high school played across Kim's face. A feeling far beyond recognition flowed through him as a memory came back to life. He would have known that smile, known Kim through it, anywhere.

"You must be the Coopers." Wayne Johnson's voice broke through the memories and startled Matt into the discovery that he had walked to the table without being aware of taking any steps. Wayne reached out and took Carol's hand. "So nice to meet you. Somehow, Eric neglected to tell us he had such a beautiful mother."

Matt stepped in closer to extend his hand to Kim, but Wayne intercepted it with a sturdy grip. "Good to meet you, too, Matt. And of course, you know Kim. Let's all sit down."

"Dad, I thought you'd sit next to Mrs. Cooper, and Mr. Cooper can sit by Mom," Julie said.

"Good idea," Wayne said. He clapped Matt on the back and steered him toward a chair. Julie's attempt to regain the introductions and social arrangements from her father had obviously failed.

Matt sat and Kim took the chair beside him. He started to speak and then saw Wayne pulling out a chair for Carol. Eric followed suit for Julie. Matt couldn't figure out any way to stand back up and hold a chair for somebody who was already sitting down. He looked at Kim who had also watched the etiquette playing out around the table. Her eyes met Matt's, and she gave a wry shrug. The smile that followed seemed meant only for him.

CHAPTER FOUR

How long does it take to convince someone to change her mind? In Carol's case, Matt had always felt that there was no answer to that question, since there was no amount of time longer than eternity. On the rare occasions when Carol did change her mind, that was exactly what happened. She changed it. Nobody changed it for her. Nobody until Wayne Johnson. It took him less than twenty minutes. Maybe it started when he asked her which of the Amana restaurants she thought had the best food. It didn't hurt when Wayne turned to her for an opinion on whether the decor should be called "rustic" or "folk." Then, he insisted that her "experience" should be used to pick a wine for dinner, and by the time Wayne poured the first glass for Carol and said, "What a wonderful idea it was to meet here for dinner," she smiled a real smile and answered, "An absolutely lovely idea."

Matt probably should have taken notes on Wayne's technique, but, in fact, it didn't seem like some artificial technique. Wayne looked straight into Carol's eyes as she spoke, and he nodded approvingly to the whole table at her answers. Kim looked on with a twinkle in her eyes as if nothing pleased her more than her sociable husband's command of the gathering.

Julie followed in her father's footsteps, engaging Matt with basketball questions and conversation at every opportunity. Her knowledge of timeout strategies, zone defenses, and little known quirks of famous coaches provided Matt an opportunity he should have relished. Instead, he wished he could call his own timeout. He didn't want to offend his beautiful, celebrity future-daughter-in-law, but he barely had time to say two words to Kim. Their conversation basically stopped at "It's been a long time."

Matt saw an opening when Julie took a forkful of apple crisp and lifted it toward her mouth. He leaned in Kim's direction, took a small breath, and said . . .

"So Matt, what do you think of our basketball expert?"

Matt could have sworn that he had started to speak, but somehow Wayne's voice came out. Across the table, Julie's smiling father sat waiting for an answer.

"Oh, well, wow. I knew she was good from TV, but I'm having a hard time keeping up with her over here." Matt didn't know whether anything he just said made any sense at all.

"That's what I think," Wayne said. "The best in the business as far as I'm concerned."

"She knows her basketball," Matt answered.

"See, honey," Wayne said to Julie. "That's a coach speaking." He tapped his coffee cup. "I keep telling her they should move her up to analyst."

"Oh, Daddy."

"Well, I mean it. A good business rewards talent. Plus, your mom and I are proud of how hard you've worked. Aren't we, Kim?"

Kim smiled at her daughter, then reached over and patted Eric's hand. "You'll have to teach your mother to brag about you as much as my husband brags about Julie."

"I completely agree with Wayne," Eric answered.

"Daddy, I think you should tell the truth," Julie said. "You really wish I did sideline reporting for football."

Wayne leaned back in his chair. "Well, that is a true man's sport. No offense, Matt."

"None taken."

"Speaking for a basketball family," Carol said to Wayne, "we are delighted to have your charming and talented daughter doing our sport."

"It's hard to argue with such an equally charming advocate." Wayne tipped an imaginary hat to Carol. "Not that I would ever abandon my own sport."

"Daddy was an all-conference linebacker at Iowa."

"See, Eric," Kim said, "he taught her to brag about him, too."

"Time for full disclosure," Wayne said. "I thought I was pretty good until I had a tryout with the pros."

"Tough?" Matt asked.

"Brutal," Wayne answered, "but it wasn't the toughness, I just had to face the fact that I wasn't talented enough."

"People have different talents," Carol said.

"I'm just glad I stayed in school and got my degree. You guys at the NCAA can't emphasize that too much, Eric. You know, of course, I became an orthodontist as penance."

"I guess I didn't know that." Eric looked from Kim to Julie to Wayne as if searching for the answer to a family riddle.

"Penance for my football career and all of the people that I hit in the mouth. In fairness, I took quite a few shots, myself."

"It hasn't slowed down his talking," Kim said with the twinkle in her eyes sparkling just a little more.

"Am I talking too much, dear? I guess I can't help it. This has just been such a wonderful night, and I'm so pleased for our kids."

"Here, here," Matt said.

The four parents raised their coffee cups in salute.

"Next time, you've got to come to our house," Wayne said. "I'd really love to have you see the place."

"I'll bet it's beautiful," Carol said. "We've got to have you over to our house, too. I was thinking all the way up here tonight about what kind of meal I could fix for the six of us. Maybe over the holidays . . ."

"Mom, you're getting a little ahead of yourself," Eric said. "Winter's the busiest time of year for both Julie and me."

"Oh, honey, I know you're right, but, Wayne and Kim, you're more than welcome. I can cook something special."

"That's an invitation that would be hard to refuse,"

Wayne said, "but I would still love to have you guys see our place. I believe I spoke first."

"I thought gentlemen were supposed to defer to ladies," Carol said.

Matt shifted in his chair. Images of the ride over before dinner began to play through his head.

"Maybe I'll try gentle persuasion, instead." Wayne smiled.

"I see, such as gently hitting me over the head like you did in your football days." Carol made air quotes and gave Wayne her I'll-smile-more-sweetly-than-you smile.

"Maybe you should just cater dinner at Wayne and Kim's house," Matt joked.

"That's a great idea!" Wayne said.

"Now dear, we can't impose like that," Kim said.

"It's no imposition at all." Carol beamed. "I can practically cater in my sleep. Plus, I'll have Matt to help me load everything."

"Actually, I was just kidding," Matt said. He looked around the table for Eric or Julie to say something. They had wisely dropped out of the conversation. Why was it that children had to end up smarter than their parents?

Wayne spoke instead. "I say a good idea is a good idea, kidding or not. Right, Carol?"

"I have to agree," she answered.

Matt glanced at Kim. With so little chance to talk to her during the meal, he had spent the evening trying to interpret the subtle changes in the smile that played across her face. Now he searched even harder for clues. However she felt about the potential onslaught of Carol armed with a stewed lamb shank or fricasseed chicken leg, Matt couldn't read Kim's current expression at all. It didn't make any difference. From the glowing enthusiasm Wayne and Carol shared, Matt knew he would be helping to schlep a five-course meal across the frozen prairies of Iowa to Cedar Rapids before the winter ended.

CHAPTER FIVE

Matt kept his arm around Carol's waist and pulled her a little closer in the cold, December night air. They waved from their front porch at Eric's and Julie's disappearing taillights. Carol had taken their early departure well. The plan had been for Eric and Julie to drive to Cedar Rapids in the morning, but Eric had checked the ever-vigilant Weather Channel right before opening presents. While the reporters assured any potential four-year-old viewers that Santa's sleigh could navigate the developing Christmas storm, Eric focused his attention on the radar map. With presents opened, cookies eaten, and snow starting to fall in Nebraska, he and Julie hit the road to join Old Saint Nick as Christmas Eve travelers.

"Let's go inside," Carol said. "I'm cold."

Matt followed his wife in the door and plopped down

in the big swivel rocker everybody knew was Dad's chair. As if demonstrating the scientific law that every action has an equal and opposite reaction, Angie stood up from the couch.

She walked over and took her mother's hand. "So they're on their way, huh?"

"I think it's a good idea." Carol stroked Angie's hair. "Your father and I didn't want them driving in snow tomorrow."

"It was a great Christmas Eve," Angie said. "Best cookies ever."

"Did you like the new ones with the chocolate mints inside?"

"Best of the best," Angie answered.

"Good enough to have another." Matt pointed toward the coffee table. "A little help?"

Angie wrinkled her nose at her father then dutifully carried the cookie tray over to his chair.

"Thank you, sweetheart." Matt took a mint melt-in-your-mouth and a mincemeat merrymaker from the remaining mound of cookies. With Carol, only too much was enough on a holiday cookie tray.

"I think I'm going upstairs," Angie said. "I still want to call Brian. Maybe later I'll email him a surprise card for tomorrow."

"I take it this is an announcement that you're retiring for the evening," Matt said.

"I guess so." Angie bent down and kissed him on the cheek. "Is that okay, Mom?"

"You go ahead, honey. I've got things to do in the kitchen."

"You need any help?"

"No, no. Everything's under control. Say 'Hi' to Brian and wish him a merry Christmas."

Matt watched quietly. Was he becoming the old man who sat in his chair and got a kiss on the cheek while the women talked business? In the moment it took to have that thought, Carol headed toward the kitchen and Angie started up the stairs. He heard Carol start water running and wondered what part of preparing the Cornish game hens for tomorrow had commenced. Traditionally, a standing rib roast graced the table for Christmas dinner. Matt loved it, Eric loved it more, Carol loved cooking it, and Angie probably wished they just would have had turkey again like Thanksgiving. With Eric gone tomorrow, Carol had decided on Cornish hens as a "cheerful change."

Nobody thought the change really was cheerful to Carol. As the water continued to run in the kitchen, Matt guessed she was probably standing at the sink crying. If so, she wouldn't want him interrupting her private moment of sadness. Carol shared her emotions like she managed most everything—on her own terms. After so many years together, Matt understood.

What he hadn't understood until now, as he sat in the neat and orderly living room, was what he must have been missing for a long time without it really sinking in. It took Eric being on his way to Cedar Rapids with his fiancée and Angie upstairs phoning her boyfriend for Matt to recognize how much he missed the Christmas Eves of his kids' childhood years. Gone was the pure anticipation of tearing the wrapping paper off a Mr. Science microscope or some Bubbly Bear bath soap. Life had moved along so gradually and evenly that, until this moment, he hadn't truly felt the loss of times like Eric and Angie setting out to build a Lego "megalopolis" on the living room floor and falling asleep before they finished.

How many times had he carried them to bed exhausted from the excitement of Christmas presents and dead to the world despite being fueled by more cookies than Carol would ever allow them to eat on any other day of the year? And how many times had he and Carol sat on the couch holding each other and saying what a beautiful Christmas Eve it had been? How long ago had those things actually happened? It seemed like only a handful of years to Matt. Had it really been more than half a lifetime for Eric and Angie? He looked across the living room at the glowing Christmas tree as if that unchanging link to those times past could answer his question.

He heard the water turn off at the sink. He hoped that meant Carol had finished her cry. Maybe they could tell each other that this had been a beautiful Christmas Eve, too. He hoped so. Matt got up and started slowly toward the kitchen.

CHAPTER SIX

Leave it to Carol to have a slow cooker that would plug into the minivan's cigarette lighter when they were ready to leave for Cedar Rapids. It sat on the kitchen counter slowly emitting the aroma of vegetables simmering in wine sauce. The seductive smell grew stronger as she lifted the lid and added perfectly browned pieces of chicken. Matt always told Carol that coq au vin was her absolute best dish. She must have thought so, too, since she chose it to take to Kim and Wayne's house.

Matt had offered to help, but Carol wanted each onion perfectly peeled and every carrot sliced to precise thickness. That didn't surprise him, knowing as he did how much she wanted to impress Eric's future in-laws. Even under ordinary circumstances, Matt found it best to keep his hands out of Carol's cooking. This time, though, he really wanted to contribute something to the meal. She did give him a peck on the cheek when he cleared away the onion skins. He could see that the frying pan needed washing. Maybe that would get him another kiss.

"There," Carol said. "We'll let that simmer until we get everything else packed up. It'll take two hours to drive over. I'm sure Wayne will want to show us around the house. Then, they'll probably offer us a drink before dinner. That should be just about ideal timing for the flavors to blend."

Carol always believed there was an exact moment when the flavor of the sauce infused the chicken to perfection. Matt actually liked the leftovers better the next day after everything had soaked together in the refrigerator. On the surface, his obvious lack of refinement might have seemed like grounds for divorce on the part of an expert cook like Carol, but what wife doesn't love a husband willing to eat leftovers?

Carol took one of her small catering coolers from its storage closet and looked in his direction. "Matt, would you be a sweetheart and get three of those cold packs out of the freezer?"

"Sure thing." He rarely saw his wife quite giddy enough to say things like "be a sweetheart."

"I can fit the salad makings in here." She patted the ice chest.

"Do you think you should have let Kim make the salad? She offered."

"She was probably just being polite. Besides, I wanted to take my pineapple Dijon dressing. It goes so well with coq au vin. I mean, how do you have someone else make a salad and then show up with a bottle of your own dressing?"

"What if somebody doesn't like Dijon?"

"Don't be silly, Matt. I'm bringing my homemade French, too."

Carol had arrayed four kinds of greens, grape tomatoes, and a cucumber on the kitchen counter. She seemed to be debating between the yellow or orange pepper in either hand.

"Maybe Kim can help you fix the salad," Matt said.

"Don't worry. I'll make Wayne do that. It was his idea to have me cart dinner to their house."

"Actually, it was my idea."

"I know that, dear," she said, "but you weren't serious. He was the one who really wanted to do it. I'll make him help. That way you and Kim can have some time to catch up. That would be nice, wouldn't it?"

"I'm not sure there was ever anything to catch up on."

"I swear, Matt. The way you talk about her makes me nervous." Carol put both peppers in the cooler.

"Nervous?"

"Yes, nervous. You definitely make it sound like she was a snob in high school."

"I keep telling you she was nice. We just didn't hang out together. Okay? It's not like I hung out with much of anybody."

"Goodness. I guess I didn't realize you hadn't gotten over high school," Carol said.

"That's not what I'm saying. Let's just drop it."

Carol turned from the counter with both hands on her hips. "I wasn't trying to make an issue out of it. I'm only thinking of Eric. She's going to be his mother-in-law. Kim certainly doesn't have much to say."

"There's nothing wrong with someone being quiet."

"Sounds like you're defending her," Carol said.

"Sounds like you're attacking her," Matt answered.

"Oh, don't be silly. It's just that Wayne and Julie are so outgoing."

"So Julie takes after her father." Matt carried the frying pan over to the sink and ran some water. He didn't particularly care anymore if Carol gave him another peck on the cheek, but he was too irked to stand stupidly next to the stove doing nothing.

"You're probably right," Carol said. "I think she looks a little like him."

"Wayne's bald!"

"I'm obviously not talking about her hair. It's her features. Especially through the eyes and her mouth, too."

"I guess I wasn't studying Wayne as closely as you were." Matt squeezed dish soap into the water. Maybe he squeezed a little too much. "You know, Kim was very pretty in high school."

"But I'll bet she wasn't the knockout that Julie is. Anyway, I've got to go upstairs and change clothes."

Matt glanced toward Carol. The kiss he didn't care about didn't happen. Of course, Carol was right. Kim couldn't compare with Julie's beauty. High school cute and TV star stunning were two different things. Matt had seen it clearly over dinner in the Amanas. Kim spoke, dressed, and presented herself quietly. It hadn't occurred to him at the time; but of the three women at the table, Julie definitely would have turned heads first and Carol would have drawn attention next. Somehow, the thought made Kim feel all the more dear to him.

Matt stared out the kitchen window. He reached in the sink, turned the strainer, and let the water slowly drain away.

CHAPTER SEVEN

Matt sat on the plaid sofa in Kim and Wayne's family room and looked across at the tennis pictures and trophies of Julie's two brothers. He couldn't think of a sport more different from football than tennis. It made Matt wonder if they chose it as a way to avoid comparisons with their highly accomplished father. Wayne definitely projected a formidable presence, so much so that he was the one to conduct the house tour when Matt and Carol arrived. For thirty-two years, Matt had ceded their house and the various apartments that led up to it to Carol's dominion. He wasn't prepared for how much it unnerved him when Kim deferred to Wayne as the tour guide for their home.

Kim did manage to assert herself when salad preparation time arrived. She had deflected Carol's plan to make Wayne help, and the two women retired to the kitchen. Of course, that also meant that the time for Kim and Matt to "catch up" vanished. Instead, a second tour, this time of Wayne's seemingly endless array of electronics, provided the men's agenda. Wayne demonstrated the most elaborate big screen TV, DVR, satellite dish, and media editing set-up that Matt had ever seen. He learned firsthand that Wayne recorded every game, anywhere in the country, that Julie worked.

Wayne's favorite creation from his impressive home media center seemed to be his compilation of Julie bloopers—the time a mascot goat on a football sideline tried to eat her windbreaker, the All-American basketball player who referred to Julie three times as Erin, the stray basketball that hit her in the rump completely unawares. Matt thought immediately of the obnoxious funny videos TV shows he hated so much, but Wayne's obvious, underlying fatherly pride made Matt smile at Julie's goofs despite himself. By the time the women called them to the dinner table, Matt had almost forgiven Wayne for not being Kim.

Matt didn't know exactly how to feel about the evening. Carol had managed to produce probably her best coq au vin ever, but even Wayne's expansive personality had difficulty filling up all the space created by the long dining room table. Matt guessed that their hosts ate in the kitchen when they didn't have company. He hoped so, anyway. It was Kim who suggested moving to the family room as a cozier place for dessert.

Dessert preparations took Carol and Kim back to the kitchen while Wayne excused himself for a "short business call." Matt hadn't anticipated the time sitting alone in the family room. He turned his attention away from the shelves of family memorabilia to watch the reflection of flames from the gas fireplace dancing on the glass patio doors. The solitude left time for reflections of his own.

Wayne had raved throughout dinner about Carol's cooking and finally exclaimed that she ought to sell her coq au vin. Carol drew on her special reserve of charm to remind him with her cutest smile and a wink that as a caterer, selling her coq au vin was exactly what she did do. In Wayne's shoes, Matt might have felt a tinge of embarrassment. Instead, Cedar Rapids' leading orthodontist launched into a soliloquy on excellence ranging from Carol's cooking to Matt's conference basketball championship to his own passion for turning profits from dentistry into successful investments and business ventures. It took a while for Wayne to get around to how much the congregation at their church loved Kim for putting out the church bulletin and working as the part-time secretary. The praise seemed so small after Wayne had pronounced Carol a world-class caterer that Matt was relieved to have arrangements for dessert change the subject. Now, he was wondering who would return first—Carol and Kim with dessert or Wayne from his phone call? The answer turned out to be a tie as his host entered from the hall carrying a tray loaded with a coffee pot and cups. The women flanked him on each side.

"Look at this," Wayne said. "The girls intercepted me and put me to work."

"Now Wayne, it's not like we made you make the coffee," Carol said, toting napkins and silverware.

"I'm sorry we left you sitting here all alone," Kim

said to Matt.

"It's quite all right. Wayne said he had business to attend to."

"My husband always has business," Kim said with a wry smile in her eyes.

"Guilty as charged," Wayne answered.

"I was enjoying the fire," Matt said. He watched Kim set the plate with Carol's lemon mousse cake on a side table. It was Carol's kind of generosity to prepare a beautiful dessert but reserve the honor of cutting the cake for their hostess. Kim carefully sliced the first piece. She placed it on a dessert plate and handed it to Matt. Carol followed with coffee, and both women worked together with a graceful ease until the four servings were complete.

"Carol, this is every bit as delicious as your coq au vin," Wayne said. "I tell you, you're just going to give me more ideas."

"Ideas?" she asked.

"My husband also always has ideas," Kim said.

"You see," Wayne started. "I've got this friend."

"He always has a friend, too."

Wayne reached over and patted Kim's hand. "Now, dear, don't make it sound like I'm up to some kind of scheme. It's just that Carol's coq au vin is so delicious. I really meant that she should sell it. I'm thinking beyond the catering. Anyway, I called my friend Randy. We own several pieces of real estate together."

Carol put down her plate. "You're very flattering, Wayne, but catering suits me much better than operating a restaurant would."

"No, no, no. I wasn't thinking restaurant. Randy and I

met through an investment group in on the real estate deals, but he owns an egg freezing plant."

"Egg freezing?" Matt said.

"Of course, they cook them first. Randy's family have been poultry farmers for years. He's got a completely integrated operation. They produce the eggs and then cook and freeze them in a plant right on their own farm."

Matt looked at the last bite of lemon mousse cake on his plate and suddenly didn't have much of an appetite.

"Who in the world wants frozen eggs?" Kim asked.

"That's the thing. All kinds of places. Fast foods, convenience stores, coffee shops. Randy makes the inside of all those breakfast sandwiches. His company is the biggest supplier in the country."

"Wayne, are you setting up a chicken and egg joke?" Carol said.

"Beg your pardon?"

"You know, which comes first? Coq au vin is obviously made from the chicken."

"No, no, no. I'm not joking at all." Wayne sat up straighter in his chair. "Randy keeps up with all the technology in food freezing. Turns out that egg freezing is not as easy as you'd think."

Matt had actually never thought about it. He looked at Kim and saw her holding in a laugh.

"You see," Wayne said, "it takes real technology to keep a frozen egg like an egg and not like a piece of rubber."

"I'm very happy for your friend's success," Carol said. She looked toward Wayne and arched her eyebrows.

Kim folded her hands in her lap and looked at Matt.

As Matt took in the whole scene, Wayne leaned toward Carol. "Let me get right to the point. I asked Randy if the technology existed to have truly gourmet frozen foods. Something that would do justice to your fabulous cooking."

"Wayne, you've only eaten one thing," Carol said.

"Doesn't make any difference. I'll bet you've got a dozen specialties just as good. Am I right, Matt?"

"I'd have to say yes, although the coq au vin is hard to beat."

"Even if that is her best, the others can't be far behind."

"Her beef stroganoff is great. Then there's the chicken cacciatore. Bavarian dinner."

"See, that's the spirit," Wayne said.

Matt did feel himself getting drawn into Wayne's enthusiasm.

"Carol's Catered Masterpieces!" Wayne exclaimed. "I can see it now, a whole line of gourmet frozen foods."

"Whoa," Carol said. "You're making an empire out of a little catering kitchen in our house."

"Not at all, Carol," Wayne said. "Your recipes. That's the empire."

Carol smiled.

"Presided over, I must add, by a beautiful empress."

Carol's smile broadened. "Oh, don't be silly."

"I'm absolutely serious. Randy said he would meet with us. No commitments. No obligation. Nothing more than fact finding."

"Wayne, I really don't know," Carol said.

But Matt did know. He could tell by the look on

Carol's face. She might as well have served her seafood paella for dinner. Wayne had set the hook.

CHAPTER EIGHT

"Dad, you really ought to weigh about three hundred pounds by now."

Matt motioned with the piece of garlic bread in his hand. "Eric, you know how your mom is. Very sensible meals ninety percent of the time."

"I remember."

They both reached for the aluminum pan of lasagna in the center of the kitchen table.

"You first," Matt said. He watched his son scoop into the pan with a large cooking spoon—a breach of serving etiquette that never would have been tolerated if Carol were home. Same for the two open beer cans on the table. Somehow, the beer tasted better straight out of the can. Maybe that was because Carol always made Matt pour his into a glass. Maybe it was just because Eric was home tonight.

"What's Mom catering tonight?"

"It's a track team reunion. I think that's why they wanted lasagna. You know, carbo-loading for old times' sake."

"Isn't February kind of a strange time for a track team?"

"They were the conference indoor champions ten years ago," Matt said. "I'd say three-quarters of your mom's business in the winter has something to do with the college. You want another beer?"

"Sure."

Matt walked to the refrigerator and opened the door. He popped open two cans of Pabst. He couldn't exactly remember when the time came that he stopped giving parental warnings about drinking and started enjoying having a beer with his son. Does everything in the world just creep up on a person?

"Your mom's sorry she had the job tonight."

"I'll see her later," Eric said. "I didn't know I'd be coming through until a couple of days ago. I'm covering this thing in Ames for another guy in the office."

"Oh?"

"Kidney stones," Eric said.

"I hear that's awful."

"That's the general impression I got. It did give me the chance to make the trip."

"If he's like most people, he probably thinks Iowa is boring, anyway."

"Kidney stones or Ames," Eric said. "I'm thinking John would have chosen Ames."

"I'm still glad you're home."

"Me, too. Julie and I are coming back in a couple of

weeks, but we're not going to make it over here."

"You're coming to Iowa?"

"Cedar Rapids," Eric said. "It's all wedding arrangements. May sixteenth isn't that far away."

Eric was right. The kids had managed to pick a date early enough not to cut into Carol's prime season for catering weddings and late enough that Angie's semester at grad school would be over.

"Just Cedar Rapids, huh?" Matt said.

"Julie has a Thursday night game in Iowa City. We spend the next day in Cedar Rapids. Then, she flies to Columbus for a Saturday game."

"Busy lady, your fiancée."

"It's basketball season. They're always like that, but we've got to get the final wedding stuff finished. We figured since she was going to Iowa City, anyway."

"Makes sense."

"Was your wedding a hassle?" Eric asked.

"I don't know," Matt said. "Your mom and your Grandma Edwards handled all that. In those days, the groom pretty much just showed up and said 'I do.' As long as he had a ring in his pocket everything was okay."

"No groomsmen's presents? No who dances with whom?"

"Not that I recall. Your mom's folks didn't have a lot of money. We didn't want them spending a lot, anyway. We had the reception in the church basement. It was nice. Small towny. You know how Emmetsburg is."

Eric pushed back in his chair. "About two months ago, we would have eloped to Emmetsburg."

"Problems?"

"Julie's dad really wanted to have the wedding at

their house. Ceremony in the garden. Reception on the lawn. Dance in the tennis court."

"What did Kim say?"

"Not much. I think she just wanted whatever makes Julie happy. That Wayne's something else. He kept talking, saying how he could hire a wedding planner. Decorate the fence around the court with thousands of lights. And I know Julie's thinking she's going to be dancing around in her wedding dress on a slab of green asphalt. I could see her mind working. Tables all over the lawn, then everybody has to file through a chain link gate to get to the dance floor."

"Not the best," Matt said.

"And if it rains?" Eric added. "But, Julie can handle her dad. So, we're having the reception at their country club. She says it's beautiful."

Matt flashed back to the times when Carol had asked him if Kim was unfriendly. It was always the same concern. What kind of mother-in-law would Kim be for Eric? Matt wondered why he had never thought of the same question about Wayne as a father-in-law.

"How about you?" Matt asked. "How do you do with Wayne?"

"I've got to say he's something else. Julie's crazy about him. She says his heart's in the right place."

"What do you think?"

Eric tapped a finger against his half-empty beer can. "I think she's right, but that's what I was saying about the dancing. You know, the bride and groom have a wedding dance with nobody else on the floor. So he's cool with that, but he says he should start and then give Julie over to me. It's like the father giving away the bride again."

"Is that the way it's supposed to be done?"

"I don't know." Eric shrugged. "Mom probably does, but it sounded okay to me."

"I guess it's settled, then." Matt got up and took their dishes to the sink.

"Yeah."

Matt turned. "Tell you what. Don't mention it to your mom just in case that's not the way it's done."

Eric carried the lasagna pan to the kitchen counter and reached into a drawer for some aluminum foil. "Mom's got us well trained, doesn't she?"

"Huh?"

"Look at us cleaning up the kitchen." Eric laughed. "Guys don't clean up, and on top of that, I have to be careful not to let something slip about this dancing situation."

"We don't have it so bad. Plus, I really don't think there's anything unmanly about cleaning up."

"No, but I do have to tell her about the dancing eventually. Julie's got the whole thing worked out. Wayne hands her to me. We dance alone. Then Wayne asks Mom to dance. And then, you ask Kim to dance. It's like . . ."

What was it like? He could hear Eric's voice, but Matt's mind had stopped on "you ask Kim to dance." Matt didn't dance. It was one of his great shortcomings in life that Carol had begrudgingly forgiven. Matt hadn't danced as an out-of-place teenager in Ankeny or in college or even at his own wedding. Now, he hadn't so much as shaken her hand yet and Matt was supposed to dance with Kim Gustafson . . . Johnson. Oh hell, Kim!

CHAPTER NINE

How long does it take to learn that people never change? Edwin Edmonds always had to make an entrance. He and Matt had been best friends for almost thirty years, and Edwin had never once been on time for anything. Matt had no reason to believe that today would be different, but that didn't make the cold feel any better standing in front of the Fine Arts Building on a Sunday morning in March. The purpose of their meeting didn't make the waiting any more comfortable, either.

Teaching Matt to dance seemed a perfect role for Edwin. Anyone on campus would have laughed and agreed, although Matt had already made Edwin promise to keep this session completely confidential. Even Carol didn't need to know. Especially Carol. Of course, there were lots of things most people didn't know about Edwin. He kept them too well hidden by his flamboyant personality.

Edwin had been Matt's unseen support in his early days as a ridiculously young and inexperienced basketball coach. Maybe unseen wasn't quite the right word for a theater professor who showed up at every home game draped in his latest winter cape. Edwin always claimed that people figured he was there to watch young men "cavort in their underwear." Almost nobody knew that Edwin had been an all-state basketball player in Ohio before going to the university to study theater. Without Edwin's advice, Matt might not have made it as a coach.

Carol and Matt's marriage received a similar boost from Edwin. He could always fix a leaky faucet, get an ancient car started, and generally solve the myriad of daily disasters facing a young married couple without the money to own things that actually worked. Apparently, the only thing Edwin never learned to do was read a clock.

The sudden opening of the front door startled Matt out of his passive annoyance into active agitation. "Jesus, Edwin. You scared the shit out of me."

"Deepest apologies."

"What the hell were you doing?"

"I was under the impression that this was to be a clandestine meeting," Edwin said. "I came in through the back door."

"Ten minutes late while I stood out here for all the world to see."

"Matty, this is a college campus. Who is likely to be awake at nine o'clock on a Sunday morning?"

"Ten after nine."

"Whatever you say." Edwin bowed and held the door. "Come in."

"Thank you."

"I thought we could use the little theater," Edwin said. "Lots of room to unleash your latent Fred Astaire."

Matt followed him down the corridor. "Don't be expecting anything latent—dancing skills or otherwise."

"I see. Destined for disappointment again."

Matt didn't answer, thinking instead about how easy it was for them to fall into their usual banter even when Edwin annoyed him.

Edwin unlocked the little theater and flipped on a light switch. "Here we are."

"Yeah, here goes nothing."

"Now, now, no need to be pessimistic. I shall soon have you ready to sweep your former high school queen off her feet."

Matt knew he shouldn't have told Edwin anything about Kim.

"Or at least," Edwin continued, "I should be able to keep you from stepping on her feet."

"Just enough to get me through one dance will be fine."

"And what of the lovely Carol? Under the circumstances, won't she expect you to take a spin or two with her?"

"Carol knows I don't dance."

Edwin held a hand to his face. "What a patient woman. Matty, you really did marry above your station."

"Right, Carol 'patient.' How long have you known the two of us?"

"Well, in this instance, at least, she seems patient.

Maybe it's a virtue she's cultivating."

"Uh huh."

"Just the same as I'm cultivating your dancing skills. Shall we start?"

Matt nodded.

"First off, you're the man. It is truly folly for me to teach you by facing you and explaining everything in reverse." Edwin turned his back to Matt. "Put your hands on my waist and just do what I do."

Matt did as he was told.

"And Matty, don't get any ideas. I know I still have a nice butt."

"You flatter yourself for an old guy," Matt said.

"I'm only five years older than you, as I recall."

"My point exactly."

"Ah, my friend, I do feel sorry for you. In some circles, men actually become more attractive as they get older."

"I'll take your word for it. Now how about that dance lesson?"

Edwin reached down to his waist. "That's right. Hands right there. I presume you want to keep this simple."

"Absolutely."

"Very good then, a garden-variety box step. Follow my feet and do what I do."

Matt started to move his feet as Edwin counted. "One, two, three, four. One . . ."

Somehow, Matt's one kept ending up on Edwin's two or three or who knew what number.

"Relax, Matty. Watch a minute and then we'll start again.

Matt's eyes traced the simple pattern repeated on the little theater floor.

"Two, three, four. Here we go again. Hands on my waist. Step together, slide. Step together, slide. That's right. Good. Good. Keep on the beat. You light up my life. You give me hope, to carry on . . . two, three, four. Da da da da. Not too hard, is it? Da da da da."

Matt smiled as his feet kept time. "No, not too bad."

"Just dance like that. Da da da da. Good good good good."

Edwin stopped and looked back. "You think you can do that?"

"Maybe for one song. I hope not that song."

"Twenty-five years ago, it would have been a lock. Trust me." Edwin turned with a flourish. "My people know these things."

"You do realize it's just the two of us here," Matt said. "You don't have to play the part all the time."

"Point well taken. But Matt, just for the record, I do truly love Judy Garland."

"I have no doubt."

"All right, back to the task at hand." Edwin stepped in closer. "You're the guy, so your arms go here. Hers go like this. See, here I am anyway, playing a part. Isn't irony delicious?"

"Is this right?"

"Perfect." Edwin reached over and punched the button on a CD player. The little theater filled with the sound of Frank Sinatra crooning "Strangers in the Night." "Here we go. You can keep it simple. Guys lead with their hips. Move in a little tighter when you want to move around the dance floor, but don't give her the prize too soon."

"Edwin!"

"Dance, Matty. Dance."

Matt started moving his feet again. "I'm dancing, okay? But, there isn't going to be any prize. The woman is going to be my . . . my . . . my whatever-in-law."

"I don't think so," Edwin said. "I believe Eric's mother-in-law is as far as the terminology goes."

"That's the point. Eric's mother-in-law. You don't need to make anything more out of it than that."

"And how many times have you mentioned this woman to me in the last three months?"

Matt didn't answer.

"Precisely," Edwin said. "I've lost count, too."

"Oh, for Pete's sake."

"Tell me this. Is she still lovely?"

Matt stopped dancing. "You don't listen, do you?"

"On the contrary. Perhaps I listen too well. Is she?"

"I guess," Matt answered. "In a different way."

"I'm sure. Matty, she'll always be lovely to you. Nothing can change what we share in our youth."

"She barely knew me."

Edwin put his arm back around Matt. "Dance. Just dance. It's no different than Adam Bealer. He barely knew me in high school, but I knew everything about him. One year, I took introductory Spanish in summer school and dropped French in the fall just so I could be in second-year Spanish with him. Now you know me, Matt. Don't you think I would have preferred French? Oh, how I wished he was gay."

"You were high school kids. How do you know he wasn't?"

"Oh, I would have known. Believe me, I would have known."

Frank Sinatra had switched to singing about "Once Upon a Time."

"So what do you think you'd do if you ever saw him again?"

Edwin pulled back a little. "Who knows . . . who knows? Be careful, Matty."

CHAPTER TEN

A coffee shop in a cornfield. Matt played Kim's words through his mind again. That's all this was when they were in high school—a cornfield. Now strip malls extended out of town along the highway all the way to the new community college campus. Matt shook his head as he laid bills on the counter to pay for a decaf, a latté, and two scones. Kim had already carried the order to their table. Earlier, they both had the same notion that they would find a coffee shop downtown. Instead, they found downtown Ankeny barely there and certainly not offering a place for coffee. He dropped his change in the tip jar and joined Kim.

"Well," Matt said, "how do you suppose our two entrepreneurs are doing?"

"Probably having the time of their lives. Wayne loves his business ventures. Carol seemed pretty enthusiastic, too."

"She is."

"What amazes me is chicken man having his plant right outside of Ankeny." Kim shrugged. "Such a coincidence."

Matt laughed and she gave him a perplexed look.

"Chicken Man," he said. "That was on the radio when we were in high school."

"Oh it was, wasn't it?" Kim laughed, too. "Do you suppose that's why I said it?"

"Could be. I loved the stupid thing. Da ta da. Chicken Man!"

"I guess I wasn't that much into it." She paused and put her hands around her mug of latté. "It was funny, though."

"Maybe more of a teenage boy thing," Matt said.

"Maybe."

"Anyway, Carol and Wayne have really dived into things."

"I know, four meetings already," Kim said. "It's been nice of Carol to make the drive to Cedar Rapids."

"She has a flexible schedule. I know Wayne has to work around his dental appointments."

"They usually have lunch at the club. He's always pumped up on those days."

"Really? You suppose we ought to be worried about those two?"

Kim put down the scone she was about to bite into. "Wayne? Oh, no. I mean, business really is business to him."

"Sorry," Matt said. "I was just kidding. Ten thousand comedians out of work and I try to be funny."

"Pardon?"

"I should have left the humor to Chicken Man."

Kim smiled.

"I am glad that they brought us along for the trip to Ankeny," Matt said.

"I'm glad they didn't make us go look at that egg freezing factory."

Matt laughed again.

"The town has changed, hasn't it?" she said.

"It was good to look around." He thought about the big box stores out along the freeway. "I couldn't believe all the stuff out by the interstate."

"Oh, I know. Best Buy, Home Depot, Staples. Who would have thought Ankeny would need a Staples? When we were in school, you went downtown to the five-and-dime and hoped they had some poster board and colored markers."

"And the lumberyard was downtown, too. Right by the tracks."

"When they still had railroad tracks," Kim said. "I never could have imagined all those big lumberyard buildings being torn down."

"No, there's not much left of the old business district."

"It's so different from when we were kids." Kim looked toward the front window.

"It is that. Of course, I was only here for high school."

"That's right. Did you come freshman or sophomore year?"

"Freshman." Matt took a drink of coffee. Had he expected Kim to remember when he moved to town? It wasn't like they had been friends in high school. He told Carol and everybody else that.

"Your dad had some kind of job that wasn't in Ankeny."

"Des Moines," Matt answered. "He was a pharmacist."

"I remember because I always wanted to live in the house you had. We only lived a block down and one street over."

"Not in high school," Matt said.

"No, before that. When I was in grade school we had one of those little 1920s bungalows, but I loved your house. Two full stories and that big porch on the front." Kim drew in the air with her index fingers.

"I thought it was just a big old square house," Matt said. "I was actually kind of embarrassed."

"Embarrassed?"

"It was right across the street from the high school. I always thought everybody could see anything that happened. I mean, Dad's undershirts on the clothesline or something."

"Your family still had a clothesline?"

Matt brushed a little crumb of scone under his plate. "No, but you get my point. You know how teenagers are."

"Easily embarrassed."

He couldn't think of anything for Kim to be embarrassed about in high school. "I always liked your house. It seemed like the rich part of town. All those new ranch-style houses. Lots of them were brick. Your neighborhood had the winding streets. *Leave It to Beaver*."

"What?" She tilted her head with the question in her eyes.

"From when we were kids. It was one of the old reruns. The ones they played at 6:30 when we got like five stations. The opening *to Leave It to Beaver*."

"Ta-ta, ta-ta-ta, ta-ta, ta-ta, ta-ta-ta, ta-ta-ta, ta-ta," she sang.

"Exactly. The opening shot with the curved streets and the nice houses. Plus, it seemed like your dad was a big shot at John Deere."

Kim shook her head. "He was in the purchasing department."

"Still, he wasn't on the assembly line like a lotta kids' dads."

"It's funny, Matt. You're talking like we were some kind of upper crust."

"That's how it felt."

"I don't think there was an upper crust in little old Ankeny. How big was it then? Ten thousand people?"

"It seemed big to me," he said.

"You're kidding again."

"Dead serious. You've never been to Garwin."

"Garwin?"

Matt shifted in his chair. "That's where we lived before. Seven hundred people."

"Sometimes it's kind of hard to conceive of, isn't it?" she said.

"Seven hundred people?"

"No, how much things have changed. I mean, this was all farmland out here." Kim looked at her watch. "You know we haven't even talked about the kids' wedding."

"Sorry, was there something we need to go over?"

"No, no, not at all." She folded her hands on the table. "This has been fun. Me wanting to live in your house. You thinking Ankeny was a big town. It was all so long ago. It's almost like we were in another life together."

CHAPTER ELEVEN

Where do the unexpected little pangs hide before they prick your heart? Does it even matter? They simply appear whenever they please. Matt's happened when the minister turned to the wedding guests and announced, "I present you the wedded couple, Julie Johnson and Eric Cooper." Obviously, the old-fashioned "Mr. and Mrs. Eric Cooper" didn't apply since Julie kept her maiden name, but Matt wasn't prepared for the little hollow place it created inside him. Maybe they could have skipped the introduction piece of the ceremony. The minister had already pronounced them husband and wife.

Introduction or not, nothing changed the fact that it was a beautiful wedding. Of course, Julie Johnson's radiance as a bride practically assured that. Over the last four months, Matt had begun to consider that Julie was the most beautiful woman he had ever met. His unspoken pride that Eric had been the one to capture the heart of such a beauty no doubt represented shallowness in Matt's character. Frankly, he didn't care. Good for Eric.

Even better for Eric, Julie seemed to be a nice person, a good person, a solid person. Last night at the rehearsal dinner, she had pulled Matt aside to talk about the song she had chosen for the first dance at the reception. She couldn't have been more earnest in her concern that Matt might not be a country music fan and wouldn't know a song by Waylon Jennings. In point of fact, she was right on both counts. Yet, something about her bit of self-consciousness at being a country music fan felt endearing in a person who talked to millions of people on TV. She must have repeated half a dozen times, "Just listen to the words." Still, with the wedding reception actually underway the words to a country song didn't seem all that important to Matt. He had greater concerns—like not stepping on Kim's feet during the song.

He looked out across the room and caught his mom's eye two tables over. Matt had no idea seating arrangements could be so complicated. Maybe that's because he never thought about it, but Julie's idea of two families coming together definitely included Matt, Carol, Kim, and Wayne sitting together. Simple math at a table for eight didn't leave room for Matt's parents, Carol's, Wayne's, and Kim's mom. That added up to nine. The younger generation failed to fill up the table because Angie was a bridesmaid at the head table and only one of Julie's brothers had a girlfriend. Eventually, Eric's best man's parents and the maid of honor's folks became the anointed couples to fill four chairs. The explanation of it all was enough to make a person's head hurt, but the Harpers and Polaceks provided excellent company. So good, in fact, that Matt forgot his nerves about dancing with Kim for at least thirty seconds.

At the sound of the wedding singer introducing himself, Matt wished he had thirty more good seconds. Instead, music from the band and Julie's and Eric's carefully choreographed approach to the center of the floor signaled the time for the first dance. Wayne joined them and quickly steered Julie a few steps around the dance floor before presenting her back to her husband. The smiling couple moved away and danced alone as the guests looked on. Suddenly, it seemed to Matt that something was missing. Then he remembered—words. Julie had told him to listen to the first song's words, but the singer wasn't singing. There weren't any words. Was there supposed to be a separate first song just for Eric and Julie before the one when Matt and Kim danced? He looked at Carol but didn't want to ask. He should have known himself. It was, after all, his only duty for the whole wedding. His chance to ask disappeared, anyway, as Wayne stepped over to Carol's chair.

"May I have the honor of this dance?" Wayne asked.

"I'd be delighted," Carol said as she stood.

Matt looked to Kim. He knew she was his partner, but nobody told him he was supposed to say something. She smiled.

"I guess it's our turn," Matt said.

"Okay." She rose gracefully from her chair.

I guess it's our turn. Maybe he just should have

asked her if she wanted to dance with an idiot.

Kim lifted her arms and Matt managed to take her hand and move into position just as Edwin had shown him. She seemed to follow his lead easily as Matt picked up the rhythm of the song. Song! Julie wanted him to listen to the words. Sometime during the haze of getting Kim to the dance floor, the singer had started singing. One section of his brain heard the lyrics, "may the arms that I seek be yours love" and another part gave an involuntary extra squeeze to his dance partner.

"Ooh!"

"Sorry," Matt said.

"It's okay."

Matt pulled back a little. Edwin was probably watching from across the room somewhere, laughing. God knows what kind of comment he would have about giving her the prize.

The song came to a blessedly quick end without Matt stepping on, squeezing, or further assaulting Kim in any way. He had no idea what the words were that Julie wanted him to listen to.

"Thank you," Kim said.

"I really don't dance," Matt answered.

"Well, you could have fooled me."

Matt looked at Wayne and Carol join together as another song began. "I guess we could try again."

"Oh, that's okay, if you don't want to." Kim edged toward their table.

"It looks like our other halves are." Matt nodded to his right.

Kim moved another step toward her chair. "Wayne will dance all night if Carol lets him."

"Carol loves to dance. I'm afraid I'm a disappointment on that score."

"They make a good couple," Kim said. "I probably should have warned her that when it comes to the fast ones, Wayne dances like an ex-football player."

"Huh?"

"A lot of energy." She twirled a finger in the air. "With any luck, nobody gets hurt."

They had reached the table and Matt pulled out Kim's chair.

"I hope you don't mind," she said. "I should go talk to my mom for a while."

"Oh, sure, that's fine."

"She's the only one of the grandparents who's alone," Kim said. "Dad died three years ago."

"I didn't think of that during the wedding." Matt touched Kim's shoulder. "I should have realized."

"Really, our families have been lucky," she said.

"Very lucky. My folks are both eighty-one. Carol's dad is, too, and her mom is seventy-nine."

"Wayne's parents are both in their eighties. It's kind of ironic. Mom's seventy-seven. The youngest of them all, and all by herself."

"I never knew your mom," Matt said.

"You must have. She helped out with almost everything when I was in school."

Matt didn't say that he was involved in almost nothing at school.

"Matt, I'm sure she'd remember you. She knew every kid in my class."

"Of course, I only went to high school in Ankeny."

"Are you sure?"

"Pretty sure." He pantomimed counting on his fingers. "Yup, four years. Just high school."

She softly tapped his wrist. "You know what I mean."

"I suppose I do."

Kim smiled. She put her hand on his elbow. "All right then, you have to come with me. I'd love to have her meet you."

CHAPTER TWELVE

"I thought you liked Kim."

"I didn't say I didn't like her." Matt stared across the kitchen table at Carol. He also didn't say how much he had always liked Kim.

"Then I don't know what the problem is," Carol said.

"I didn't say it was a problem. I only asked why we're all going to Ankeny again."

"Wayne and I have a meeting at Randy's office. Wayne wanted Kim to ride over with him. What's she going to do while we're meeting? Sit there and listen to us talk about frozen food?"

"What am I going to do?"

"Have coffee with her again. Would that be so horrible?"

The microwave dinged and Carol got up to retrieve her oatmeal. Matt couldn't understand how anyone who cooked as well as Carol could stand to eat that awful instant oatmeal for breakfast. He did understand that Carol would never have thought of asking him to go at all if she and Wayne didn't need somebody to entertain Kim. Something about that annoyed him more than it should have. He liked the idea of having coffee with Kim.

"Matt, are you listening?" Carol asked over her shoulder.

"Thinking."

"What is there to think about?" Carol poured skim milk on her oatmeal and returned to the table.

"Why, exactly, did you say Kim is going?"

"It's pretty simple, dear. Wayne likes her company on the drive over. I think that's kind of sweet."

"Right. It's darling."

"God, you're crabby this morning. A trip to Ankeny wouldn't kill you. Maybe you could be a little more like Wayne and look forward to spending a little time with your wife."

"We spend lots of time together." Matt reached for the morning paper.

"You mean like right now when I'm trying to talk to you and you decide to read the newspaper? Or like last night when you wouldn't watch the show I was watching?"

Matt put down the paper. "You know I hate doctor shows. Everybody running around in bloody scrubs, and then you hear about a tumor and then Alzheimer's and then, I don't know what, terminal ear wax."

Carol laughed. "I don't think they've ever had an episode about terminal ear wax."

"Well, you get my point." Matt smiled.

"You don't have to go, but I don't know what Wayne's going to tell Kim."

"I didn't say I wouldn't go."

"What is it, then?" Carol asked. "What's really bothering you?"

Matt looked away. He was pretty sure nothing good could come of telling Carol what was really on his mind. Maybe he didn't even know, himself, what he thought about seeing Kim after so many years. He couldn't explain why he felt so close to her when they had moved in such separate orbits as teenagers.

"Earth to Matt," Carol said.

He searched for something to say. "I guess . . . I guess it's this whole business thing."

"I know it's a big step, but we aren't taking any financial risk at all."

"Don't you think there's always risk in a business?"

"Matt, we've gone over it all. We get part ownership just for my recipes."

"I know. I know. We don't put any money in."

"I wish you wouldn't say it like that."

"I don't mean anything."

Carol pushed aside her bowl. "I understand this is all new, but that's part of it. The kids have been gone for almost ten years. Eric more than ten. Matt, I didn't realize how much I was ready for something new. Plus, I trust Wayne."

"I just don't know how it's all going to work."

"Don't you see?" Carol asked. "That's part of the fun. Part of the challenge. As far as the day-to-day, Randy's got a building lined up in Ankeny to get started in. That's where the plant's going to be. It's not like I'm going to be doing the cooking."

"Doesn't that seem strange to you? I'm used to your food coming from a kitchen, not a plant."

Carol got up and came around the table to kiss Matt on the cheek. "That's sweet. You're protective of my food. We've already talked this through completely, and everybody is committed to making this a truly gourmet line of food. We want somebody to be able to warm up a meal and have it be just like I made it."

"Doesn't sound possible."

"I think you're going to be surprised. I was really impressed with Randy's technical staff the first time we met. Plus, we've got quality control. They're going to ship me random samples of each product. I'll warm them up to be sure everything's right."

"How often?" Matt asked.

"I don't know. We have to work that out. Often enough to make sure that I'm satisfied. You want more coffee?"

Matt handed her his cup. "So we're going to have boxes of frozen food showing up at our house every day. What are we going to do with a thousand frozen dinners?"

"Entrées, Matt. We are selling gourmet entrées, and they're not going to send us a thousand. Besides, I'm going to test them. We don't have to eat it all."

Matt looked at the cup of black coffee Carol slid in front of him. Maybe he didn't know exactly what he was feeling about Kim, but, after thirty-two years, he knew precisely how Carol felt about wasting food. He could see an endless string of lunches and dinners from frozen gourmet entrées stretching out in front of him. What did Eric say to him about weighing three hundred pounds? With all the frozen beef stroganoff that lay ahead, maybe coffee and rolls with Kim in Ankeny would just be the first step down the road toward three bills.

CHAPTER THIRTEEN

"I think knowing where my food comes from is one of those things in life I could skip." Matt turned on his blinker and pulled out of the driveway for the Finest Farms egg processing plant. Having coffee with Kim had become a ritual every time Carol and Wayne had a meeting in Ankeny.

"Agreed," Kim said.

"Of course, in this case, I suppose the chickens would just as soon keep the matter private, too."

Kim put her hand to her mouth and covered a chuckle.

"Luckily," Matt said, "you got us out of there before we had to find out."

Kim shrugged. "I only said we had a lot to catch up on."

"Do we?" This was their fourth time for coffee

together. Four minutes probably would have sufficed to cover all their shared past from high school. Matt didn't understand why it felt like so much more. That Kim seemed to share the feeling surprised him most of all.

"Can we drive by the high school?" she asked.

"Sure, if you want."

"Not the new building. The old one where we went."

"It's funny," Matt said. "I knew that's what you meant."

"High school probably only has one meaning to us."

Matt stopped for a red light.

"You're a good driver," Kim said. "You're not rushing all the time like it's some kind of race."

"We've got two hours to kill in Ankeny. That's probably the definition of no need to rush."

"Oh."

"I mean, I enjoy the time . . . I wasn't saying . . . what I meant to say . . ."

This time Kim laughed out loud. She tapped a finger to her temple. "I think what you were trying to say is that you didn't know it would be so much fun to get together like we do."

Matt looked at Kim, calmly waiting for him to answer. He wondered where the confidence and control she possessed in Ankeny went to that first night at the restaurant in the Amanas or at the kids' wedding or even in her own home.

"Well, am I right?" she asked.

"Not exactly. I always thought it would be fun."

"Maybe I'm projecting a little. I wasn't completely sure about coming over with Wayne the first time. It's not you. I don't get together with people very often."

"You don't?"

"I like my house. I see people at the church office. That usually feels like enough."

"I'm glad you added our coffee dates to your list."

"Me, too," Kim said. "Very glad. It's just like back in high school."

"Huh?"

"You were always one of the smart ones. You probably knew right away it would be fun to have these get-togethers."

"I don't know about the smart part. Speaking of high school." He nodded toward the cream brick school building on the left and pulled over to the curb. "Is this okay?"

"Fine," she said. "I don't know why I wanted to come here. There's something about the fall that makes me more nostalgic."

"I think that's true for most people," he answered. "Me, anyway."

"It's the smell of the leaves. How blue the sky is. I always loved the football games around this time in October, before it got too cold."

"Those were fun. Of course, I liked basketball best."

Kim shook her head. "Definitely football."

"Because of Wayne, I suppose," Matt said.

"Not Wayne. I liked football better before I ever met him. It was the cheerleading uniforms. They were different for football. I felt so self-conscious in the ones they made us wear for basketball."

"Why? You were, without question, the cutest girl in school. Probably in all of Iowa."

"Don't be silly."

"Who's being silly?" he said. "When you guys did one of those cheers where you made a pyramid, you were always the girl at the top. That's where the cutest girl goes. You can't argue with that logic."

"I wasn't interested in logic at the time. We had those little short outfits. They made me feel like all the guys were looking up my skirt."

"Well, we were, of course."

"Matt," Kim blurted.

"Probably half the girls, too."

"Matt!"

"Sorry. You were awfully cute."

Kim shifted on the seat and smoothed her slacks. "Maybe we should get going."

"I really didn't mean anything," Matt said.

"It's not you," she answered. "Memories—they're funny things. That was a good time. A fun time, but you wouldn't really want go back again. Me, anyway. Does that make any sense?"

"I wasn't exactly the kind of high school celebrity that you were, but I think I know what you mean. You look at your life and it's been good, but you wouldn't want to do it all over another time. It's like maybe it wouldn't all turn out as well the second time, or all the surprises would be gone, or knowing the bad parts that were coming wouldn't let you enjoy the good parts."

"I don't know why, Matt, but you have a way of saying something, and it'll be the exact thing I'm thinking." She cocked her head and bit her lip. "I don't know many people that happens with. At least, not the same way. It's special. You're special."

Matt held his foot on the brake but didn't put the car

in gear. An uncertain silence hung in the air.

"Maybe it's just my fall nostalgia talking," Kim said.

"No, I know what you mean. Sometimes you say something just as it flashes through my mind." Matt paused. "Of course, it could just be from some kind of brainwashing they did on us when we were in school."

Kim smiled and shook her head.

"It was only a thought," Matt said. "Suppose we should get that coffee?"

"Excellent idea."

He skipped the highway and steered his way through residential streets on the five-minute drive to their regular coffee shop. Orange and yellow maples lined the way as they silently watched the familiar houses slide by. They parked and Matt held the front door of the shop for her as the aroma of ground coffee drifted out to meet them. A thin, stoop-shouldered kid looked up as they approached the counter.

"Can I help you?" he asked.

Kim looked at Matt, and he gave their customary order. "I'll have a medium decaf, and Kim will have a skim latté with one shot of hazelnut. Give us two scones, too."

"So you want two scones," the kid repeated back, "and two of what else?"

"Nothing," Matt said.

"No coffee?"

"Yes," Matt answered. "I mean, yes we'll have coffee. A decaf for me and a latté for her."

"With how many shots of what?"

Matt held up one finger. "One hazelnut."

"But just one decaf," the kid said.

"That's right," Matt said. He looked at Kim and wondered how many people the kid was seeing. So far as Matt could tell, he and Kim were the only people standing at the counter. Regardless, the kid seemed to be having trouble dealing with complex numbers like one and two.

"Can I have a name?" the kid asked.

"Matt."

"Okay, have a seat."

Kim and Matt walked over to the black leather sofa where they sat the last time they had coffee. They settled into opposite corners of the couch and tried to hold back a laugh.

"What was his problem?" Kim whispered.

"He looks like a student. Probably has a calculus test on his mind."

Kim let a quiet laugh slip out.

"Maybe he's a computer guy working with binary code," Matt said. "He seems to be stuck on one and two."

"Matt, stop." Kim kept laughing.

"Okay, okay," He reached over and touched her arm in mock concern. "Calm yourself."

"I can't help it," she said. "When did you get like this?"

"Like what?"

"Funny. I don't remember you joking around like this when we were kids."

"Is it a good funny?"

"It is," she answered.

"Matt!"

He turned his head toward the sound of his name

being yelled from the counter. "I better go get that."

He walked to the cash register and fished into his wallet for a twenty-dollar bill. As he waited through the ordeal of the kid making change, Matt looked back to Kim watching him from the couch. He took in her smile and thought about what he would have given to be sitting alone with her at a table all the way back in high school. He wondered if this was even better. He knew that the next two hours would melt away in warm, comfortable conversation. In some way that he didn't understand, he could see the same thought in Kim's smiling eyes.

CHAPTER FOURTEEN

Can two words make a person old? Matt didn't feel old. He could still shoot a basketball even if he couldn't really jump to rebound one. His mind told him he was twenty-five even if his body said fifty-five. But, the words *Grandpa Cooper*—those made his age real no matter what his mind said.

Eric and Julie had shared the good news during Thanksgiving dinner. Last year the engagement. This year a baby on the way. Matt hoped maybe next year at Thanksgiving dinner Eric would announce that he had won the lottery. Technically, Julie made the announcement about the baby since she actually spoke the words, and maybe it was "over" rather than "during" dinner, since the food was on the table but nobody had started to eat. If "over" was the right word, Matt could count on Carol to correct him the first time he told somebody the story. Meanwhile, he could try to sort out why he felt so happy for Eric and Julie and, simultaneously, so unnerved by the two words *Grandpa Cooper*.

Right now, he had more immediate things than his feelings to sort out. Carol had sent him to the attic to locate Eric and Angie's bassinet, the folding stroller the kids had ridden in, or anything useful from infancy thirty years ago. As he sat on the attic floor, the whole mission seemed a dubious undertaking. He already had rejected the kids' crib as an affront to current child safety standards. The old stroller had been light and handy, but Matt figured Eric and Julie would want one of those huge new models that looked like an SUV for a baby.

The more he searched, the more the trip to the attic had taken on an air of irrelevancy, particularly given Carol's current endeavor downstairs. She had led him to the cedar chest to see her idea about a Christmas present for the baby-to-be. Matt hadn't remembered Eric's "Uncle Sam" baby sleeper until Carol pulled it out. The new baby was due in May, and Carol figured that by the Fourth of July the sleeper should fit a two-month-old perfectly. She also gushed about having something Eric wore as a baby that could be "gender neutral" in the case of either a boy or a girl. Uncle Sam seemed pretty much like a guy to Matt, but he kept that thought to himself. He supposed that patriotism could be said to have no gender boundaries, and he knew better than to argue with Carol's motherly, and now grandmotherly, instincts.

The two fuzzy ball tassels on the sleeper's toes did deal a temporary blow to Carol's fun. One had a few tiny flecks of stain on the tips of the white yarn. Matt marveled that any substance could have escaped Carol's meticulous laundry skills, but whatever it was had turned brown with age. While he went to the attic, she headed immediately to the laundry room in search of stain removers.

The more Matt thought about the baby on the way, the more he wished Carol hadn't come up with the idea of a Christmas gift. He didn't believe in jinxes, never paid attention to people talking about tempting fate, didn't wear a lucky tie when he coached, and always changed his socks regularly, even in the midst of a long winning streak. He had essentially lived his life superstition-free. Still, looking at the white bassinet in front of him reminded Matt that he had only cared about one thing when Eric and Angie were on the way. Boy or girl didn't matter. Eye color didn't mean a thing. People could say the newborn looked like him or Carol or a wrinkly raisin. All he ever wanted was a healthy baby and a safe delivery for Carol. Should there be a present under the Christmas tree for a baby who wasn't born yet? He decided to knock on every piece of wood he could find on Christmas Eve.

The present probably wouldn't trigger even the slightest concern in Eric or Julie's thoughts. They had planned the new arrival so rationally and practically that the idea of luck in any form, good or bad, virtually vanished. They wanted to start a family right away because they had each passed thirty. They timed the pregnancy to get Julie through most of the basketball season on TV before she started to show. The baby would be six months old before she had to go on the road again, and the network had agreed to assign her only weekend games for the next season. That way, either she or Eric would be home with the baby every night. Matt couldn't decide whether to be more impressed with their planning or Julie's status to be able to call her own shots with a television network.

Of course, even expectant parents with the best planning find out that control only extends so far. Eric had confided to Matt after Thanksgiving dinner that Julie's stomach was teaching them that lesson. Matt knew already. He had seen her push a small portion of turkey around her plate without really eating any and pick slowly at some mashed potatoes with a tiny dollop of gravy on top. In a depiction of stereotypes that felt a little too sad to be funny, Julie did visit the relish tray twice for pickles and ate a scoop of vanilla ice cream for dessert while everyone else enjoyed Carol's pies.

"Honey, how you doing up there?" Carol's footsteps on the attic stairs accompanied her voice.

"Okay," Matt answered. "You?"

She made the last step and held up the star-spangled sleeper. "I gave up on washing out those stains. Look."

"I don't see any stains."

"Of course not. Look closer." She held a toe of the sleeper closer to him.

"No stains."

"You're hopeless," Carol said. "They wouldn't come out so I replaced the tassels. These are better. The old ones were white. See these? Red, white and blue. I had them in one of my sewing boxes."

"Good," Matt answered.

"Is that all you can say?"

"Great?"

"I swear." She put her hands on her hips. "I think they're perfect."

"Okay, I'll go with perfect . . ."

"But?"

"No buts," Matt said. "I agree."

"Matt, I know you. There's something on your mind."

Carol did know him, but there was no way he wanted her to know what he had been thinking. He didn't even want to think the words "tempting fate," much less say them out loud.

"Come on," she prodded.

"I was thinking. That's all."

"About?"

"Nothing."

"Well, it had to be something."

"It's stupid, Carol." He searched for something more to say. How hard should it be to come up with something stupid?

"Dear, this conversation is getting stupid. Just say it for heaven's sake."

"Okay . . . I was just thinking . . . when Julie told us she's expecting . . ."

"Yes?"

"It was at Thanksgiving dinner," he said.

"I remember. I was there."

"Well, here's the thing. We hadn't started eating yet."

"That's the thing?" Carol said.

"That's what started me thinking. I mean, technically, did she tell us over Thanksgiving dinner or during Thanksgiving dinner?"

"What!"

"Well, dinner was on the table even though we weren't eating it yet."

Carol placed her hand against the side of her face. "What difference could it possibly make?"

"Simple. I'll be telling the story to someone, and if I say she told us during dinner, you'll probably correct me and say it was over dinner. So I just thought I should get it right."

"Matt, are you listening to yourself?"

He shrugged.

"Do I really do things like that?" she asked.

"You correct my English."

Carol shook her head. "You really take the cake sometimes. Are you losing it in your old age? Say during dinner if you want to, or what was the other one?"

"Over," he answered.

"By all means, say over if you prefer."

"I think over is better."

"Whatever. I'm going downstairs and make some coffee. There are times, dear, when you drive me crazy."

Matt fought off the urge to say "short trip."

"You want some?" she asked.

"Maybe I could use a cup."

Carol took his hand to help pull him up from his seat on the floor. "I don't think there's any maybe about it."

CHAPTER FIFTEEN

"Oh, Matt," Carol said, "I wish I was there."

"I know, dear."

Carol picked up the morning paper and rattled a few pages. "Where's the Sudoku?"

"I did it." He pointed at a section of newspaper on the living room coffee table.

"When?"

"This morning."

"Oh."

"You never do the Sudoku," Matt said.

"That doesn't mean I wouldn't want to sometime." She dropped the paper and sagged back into the blue wing chair where she always sat.

"I would have saved it for you."

"Oh, who cares about a puzzle. I wish I was there. I'm sure I could help."

"This is Kim's time," Matt said.

"Don't you mean Julie's time? She's the one who had the baby."

"I only meant that we all agreed that Kim and Wayne should be there right now. After all, Kim is Julie's mother."

Carol got up and walked to the front window.

"We did all agree, didn't we?" he asked.

Carol turned abruptly. "I went along. I wouldn't say that I agreed."

"I don't think that Julie and Eric wanted a lot of hubbub right after the baby was born, that's all."

"What hubbub? We could have easily driven to Indianapolis."

"I think it's just the extra people."

"Nobody had to be extra people. It's not like we couldn't get a hotel room, go to the hospital and see the baby. What in the world is so extra about that? We're grandparents, too. What is extra about that?"

He didn't answer. Sometimes with Carol, there were questions that were better not to answer. The wrong answer only dug a deeper hole, and he knew that no answer would be right.

"Matt? Are you listening to me?"

"Every word."

"What's that supposed to mean?"

"It means that I understand that you want to be there."

"You see," she said, "you don't understand. Men don't understand about babies. You've never had one. Men think you simply pop one out and then go on about your business."

"I don't think that at all."

Carol waved her arm. "Well then, why don't you want to be there? This is our first grandchild, and now when he's so tiny and special, here we are sitting in our living room in Iowa."

"Eric sent us those pictures from his cell phone."

"Cell phone! You don't even like cell phones. How many times have you told me you wouldn't even have one if it weren't for basketball? Do you possibly think seeing a picture from somebody's cell phone is like holding a little baby?"

Another question better not to answer.

"You know, Matt, there are some chances you never get back in life."

"Carol, we're going down to see the baby in two weeks."

"You know what? You're so good at proving my point. Men don't know anything about babies. You have no idea how much a baby changes in two weeks. Sometimes I wonder if you care. I mean, you don't even call the baby by his name." She turned and marched past his chair. "I'm going in the kitchen."

Matt watched her leave and tried to assess who she was most mad at. Him? Eric? Kim? Julie? The world? He settled on the universe. Carol had a well-honed capacity for anger. In that regard, he had always appreciated the fact that there weren't too many things that set her off. Unfortunately, the last year had proven that several of them related to the role of mother-in-law.

He hoped that wasn't the reason Julie didn't want them to come to Indiana until later. He didn't think it was. What Eric told them made sense. Julie wanted to have her own mom to help right after the baby was born, and then the new parents wanted a few days by themselves with the baby. It sounded to Matt like the way any young couple would want things.

Carol's crack about not calling the baby by name started to sink in. She hadn't used little Matt's name either. It seemed like everybody was still calling him "the baby." The whole name thing took some getting used to, and Matt thought he had as much right as anybody to be a little slow in adjusting. He was honored when Eric and Julie announced that the baby's name would be Matthew Wayne Cooper, but he knew right away it would raise a family issue to be sorted out. Privately, he didn't think a child growing up would really like to be called "little Matt" at every family gathering. On the other hand, Matt had no desire to be known as "old Matt" from now until eternity. He didn't want to be selfish, but he had decided already to work for "little Matt" and "big Matt" to join the family lexicon rather than "young Matt" and "old Matt."

Chances were excellent that the multiple Matt issue would sort itself out with minimal pain. The Matthew Wayne pairing in Matthew Wayne Cooper nettled a little more. Matt liked Wayne. He really did. What Matt had started not to like so much was sharing things with Wayne. Sharing a name was just the latest. For the last year, it seemed Matt had shared Carol with Wayne. Matt had no idea why a dentist needed to be so involved in the start of a frozen food venture, but Wayne was. He and Carol seemed to have more meetings than a Quaker congregation.

The meetings weren't all bad. Those when Matt and

Kim tagged along to slip away for coffee were the good meetings, but more often than not, it was just Carol going off to Cedar Rapids to plan one more thing with Wayne. Something about it all made Matthew Wayne a combination of names that Matt didn't love.

On the flip side, his friendship with Kim had become more than he ever expected. They talked so easily and shared the same thoughts so often that Matt couldn't find a good word for it or even the right way to describe it. He couldn't explain how four years of high school with not much in common could create such a special connection more than three decades later. Sometimes, when he was talking with Edwin, Matt called Kim his "new old friend." Whatever it was, it made Matt happy. Now, if there was only some way to make Carol happy. He got out of his chair and walked to the kitchen.

"Whatcha doing?" he asked.

Carol stood at the counter with her back to him. "Fuming."

He slipped behind her and put his arms around her waist. "Suppose I should turn on the range hood?"

"Matt, am I like this all the time?"

He nuzzled against her neck. "You mean sexy goddess of the kitchen?"

"No, I mean bitchy."

"I understand why you're upset," he said.

"Do you? Do you really?" She turned around to face him.

"I do. Really. I know how much this means to you. You have always been probably the best mother in human captivity. Now you want to be the best grandmother."

"I just want to see our grandson." She put her arms around him.

He stroked her hair. "We will. We will."

"I know." She stepped back and brushed a tear from her cheek. "I'm not going to cry. I know Julie needs her own mother there."

"She does, and it would make a little bit of a production for us to come in from out of town even if we didn't want it to be."

"Maybe." Carol stiffened.

"I only mean it's not the same as if they lived around here and we could just drive over to the hospital."

"Let's not talk about it anymore," she said. "I'm not sure it's helping."

"Okay."

She walked over to the refrigerator and opened the freezer compartment. "What should we have for dinner?"

"What are the choices?" Matt asked.

"I have to test the lasagna and the moussaka this week," she answered. "I was thinking moussaka if you don't mind. It's got the eggplant in it. I want to make completely sure that freezing the eggplant is working out."

"Moussaka it is," he said.

The parade of frozen entrées for dinner had begun. As he had guessed, there was no way that Carol would simply sample the food for quality and let the rest go to waste. This was the Carol he knew. Maybe she had been a little bitchy today, and maybe he didn't like sharing the baby's name with Wayne, and maybe all those frozen food meetings between Wayne and Carol still seemed a little much to Matt; but, at this moment, it was good to have his real wife back.

CHAPTER SIXTEEN

The cool morning air in Carol's rose garden felt good to Matt after the long August hot spell that ended over the weekend. Still, it seemed a little ridiculous for him to be holding his cell phone and sitting on an ornamental cast iron bench surrounded by heat-stressed flowers. He should have gone to one of the upstairs bedrooms, but he hadn't thought it out clearly. All he knew was that he had to get away from Carol.

He could blame Wayne for that. He was the one who came up with the idea of a conference call. The plan worked fine for Wayne and Kim on the phone system in the dentist office. They had a speaker phone. Matt had to get on his cell while Carol used the land line. The echo between the signals made fingernails on a chalk board seem like a lullaby. Matt left the room but lost his connection. Now Wayne was trying to patch everything back together.

The conferring part of the call made actual sense. Eric and Julie's childcare crisis had come out of the blue, and the four grandparents needed to work out some kind of a solution pronto. Eric had left last night for a conference in conjunction with the Pan American Games in Mexico City, and suddenly, Julie's network wanted her at the Games, too, for the basketball broadcasts.

A person wouldn't think that international basketball could come in conflict with frozen lasagna, but Carol and Wayne had product launch events in Chicago, Milwaukee, Minneapolis, and Des Moines over the precise days that both Eric and Julie needed to be gone. At four months old, little Matt couldn't exactly hold down the fort in Indianapolis by himself. Big Matt sat on his bench and waited for Wayne to bring Carol back on the line.

"Hello," Wayne said. "Carol, can you hear me?"

"Loud and clear."

"How about you, Matt?"

"Right here."

"No interference this time?"

"I'm out in the garden," Matt answered.

"Kim, you say something," Wayne said.

"Hello."

"Is that good?" Wayne asked. "Loud enough?"

"It's fine," Carol said.

"Perfect," Matt added.

"I guess we have a situation, don't we?" Wayne said. "Everybody up to speed?"

Carol came on the line. "Partly. Eric explained things pretty fast. He was already at the airport."

"It took him a while to reach us," Matt said. "We were out to supper last night."

"Good spot?" Wayne asked.

"Yeah, a new Mexican place."

"Boys," Carol said, "we don't need any restaurant reviews right now."

Kim chuckled in the background.

"This Schuler woman," Carol said. "I didn't understand exactly what she's got to do with it."

"Annie Schuler," Wayne said. "She's the other sideline reporter for basketball. She got herself in the news for making some comments about immigration laws."

"I didn't see that," Matt said. "Something bad?"

"Didn't seem that bad to me," Wayne said, "but not the sort of thing that makes a network want to send you to Mexico City."

"I don't understand why Julie has to take her place," Kim said.

"Sweetie," Wayne said, "Julie's the top sideline reporter they've got. From what I understand, they're trying to build up the profile of the Pan Am Games, make them into a big TV event if they can. They'd probably rather have Julie than Annie Schuler, anyway."

"TV's always trying to build something up," Kim said. "Julie was supposed to have this time off."

"TV is TV," Carol said. "It doesn't sound like they're giving her much choice about going."

"That's it in a nutshell," Wayne said.

"Then we're going to have to figure out what to do," Carol said.

"We talked to Julie about getting little Matt up here,"

Wayne said, "but there's barely time and her flying from Cedar Rapids to Mexico City got too complicated. What it basically comes down to is this, somebody has to get in a car or catch a flight and be in Indianapolis tonight. Kim can go but you don't want to drive all that way by yourself, do you, sweetie?"

"I could," she said.

"I know, but you don't like to travel alone," Wayne said.

"Not really."

"Well, Wayne, I can go," Carol said. "Maybe we'll just have to cancel the product launch or you do it on your own."

Matt listened quietly. He knew Carol would want to go take care of the baby. So far they had only made one trip to see little Matt.

"Oh, Carol, we can't do that. You're the star," Wayne said. "I'll check flights from Indianapolis to Chicago. After I get Kim down there, I'll fly up the next morning. Matt, can you drive Carol to Chicago instead of her and I going together?"

"My schedule's free," Matt said. "Eric said it's only three days until he can come back."

"Okay, then," Wayne said. "It's Carol and Matt to Chicago and Kim and I to Indianapolis. I've got meetings with wholesalers in Minneapolis and Chicago, but I should be able to fly back and forth for those. I don't want Kim by herself in Julie and Eric's condo all night. I'll work on my tickets and Carol, you and Matt are going to have to come by here to pick up that promotional stuff I got ready for the trip."

"Honey, this sounds awfully complicated," Kim said.

"I could go to Indianapolis by myself," Matt said.

"Hold on," Carol said. "I love you, dear, but the thought of you taking care of a four-month-old baby by yourself is about as scary as little Matt going to Mexico City."

"Thanks."

"I'm just saying."

Carol was right, of course, but Matt didn't think she needed to broadcast it to Kim and Wayne.

"Is there any reason why Matt and I can't go to Indianapolis?" Kim asked. "He's free. I'm free. And everyone else has something important to do."

Four voices went silent.

"Matt, would that be okay with you?" Wayne finally asked.

"Perfectly fine."

"Carol, what do you think?" Wayne asked.

"Sounds like a solution to me. But Kim, I have to warn you, when the kids were here two weeks ago, he didn't even change a single diaper. You'll have to teach him everything."

"Not true," Matt said. "I am a completely competent driver."

"About babies, Kim," Carol answered. "Trust me, you'll have to teach him everything about babies."

"It'll be my pleasure," Kim said. "I'll call Julie and tell her what we worked out."

"I'll get packed," Matt said. "See you in a couple hours."

CHAPTER SEVENTEEN

Wayne kissed Kim and then opened Matt's passenger door for her. He bent down beside the car as she buckled up. "You two have a safe trip. Thanks for doing this, Matt."

"Not a problem," he answered. "You and Carol knock 'em dead . . . not literally, of course. I imagine that would be no good in the food business."

"Believe me," Wayne answered. "I've been through that plant from top to bottom. I've seen all the inspection reports. Their record for food handling procedures is perfect."

"Honey," Kim said, "I think Matt's only kidding."

"Oh . . . right. I only, well, I didn't want anybody worrying. Anyway, you two have a good trip."

Kim pulled her door shut as Matt started the engine. He backed out of the driveway and headed south.

"Here we go," Kim said.

"I guess I said the wrong thing."

"Don't worry about it. Maybe you can tell Wayne's a little excited about the start up. This is a really big thing for him."

"For all of us, I suppose," Matt said. He turned onto First Avenue toward downtown Cedar Rapids.

"He's always had his investments," she said, "but this is the first time he's ever had an active role in a business."

"He's got a good practice."

"That's different for him. Being a dentist is a service. Now there's something actually being made and sold. To Wayne, that's what a real business does."

"I didn't expect him to be so involved," Matt said. "I don't see how he finds the time."

Kim laughed. "If nothing else, my husband has energy. To tell you the truth, it's been good for him."

"Carol, too."

They drove through the downtown looking at the "For Rent" signs scattered everywhere in storefront windows. The number of empty buildings stood as silent evidence of the huge flood that a massive cleanup afterwards couldn't completely hide.

"Do you think things will ever come back down here?" Matt asked.

"I don't know. It's hard to believe how devastating it was."

"The buildings look good."

"I'm not sure that's enough," Kim said. "It had a lot of vacancies before the flood. I don't know if anybody is sure what to do with a downtown these days."

Matt pulled onto the interstate and got up to speed. "It must have been different when you worked for the Chamber."

"So different. That was a long time ago."

Matt realized that he and Kim had never talked about the years she worked for the Chamber of Commerce. They'd gone to coffee together every few months and shared such easy conversation that Matt didn't consider the things that never came up. Their talk was family, high school in Ankeny, Eric and Julie's wedding, the baby, frozen food jokes, or flower gardens. He wondered now why they hadn't filled in more of the blanks about all those years when they hadn't seen each other.

"Nice day," Kim said.

He looked out the windshield at the first of many cornfields to come. "Why'd you leave?"

"Beg your pardon?"

"The Chamber of Commerce. Why'd you leave?"

"Oh, I don't know."

"To start a family?"

"That was part of it." Kim ran her fingers up and down the seatbelt shoulder strap. "Wayne and I were thinking about it."

"But you left before?"

"I did," she said.

The countryside flew by at seventy miles an hour. "I guess I'm being nosy."

"No, no. It's just something I haven't talked about much."

"You didn't like it?" he asked.

"Honestly? I didn't like me."

"What?"

"Me. I don't want to sound conceited, but they only hired me because I was pretty."

Matt wanted to agree about how pretty she had been, but he knew that wasn't the right thing to say.

"I had a college degree, of course," she said, "but I could tell that's not really why they wanted me. Every chamber had some version of a cute young thing. It dresses up events."

"Aren't you being a little hard on yourself?"

"Yes. And on the Chamber, too, but that was part of it. I saw it at every meeting I went to." She shifted on the seat and looked toward him. "I also saw the cute women getting older and using more makeup and buying fancier clothes and doing everything they could to stay young and pretty."

"You're still pretty."

"That's sweet, even if it's not true."

"Now you're being silly," he said. "It is true."

"But I'm not young."

"Who is?"

"That's the point. I saw all these other women layering on the makeup, dyeing their hair, wearing higher heels, and they were, I don't know . . . they were brittle. That's not who I wanted to be, and I was already on the way."

"Then you were smart," Matt said.

"I guess. I know sometimes Wayne wishes I was still that other person. He thinks I should do more things. Socialize more. Have more friends."

"You had more friends than anybody in high school."

"You find things out about yourself," Kim said. "I got away from Ankeny, and that's not who I was. I didn't need to be in everything. Didn't want to. I love our kids. I have my garden. Putting together the church bulletin is fun. I answer the phone there three mornings a week and try never to get involved in church politics. Believe me, there's plenty if I let myself."

Matt pulled into the passing lane and steered around a semi hauling new cars. He glanced at a highway mileage sign as they cleared the truck.

"Long trip to Indianapolis," she said.

"I think I probably made it longer."

"Not at all," she answered. "Wayne's right about me not having many friends. I don't mind that. I even like it, but it's been nice to have your friendship. You're always so easy to be with. I think a good friend is better than just a lot of friends."

"Me, too."

"I've never told you," she said, "but I always feel a little sad when our coffee dates are over and we're headed home."

He glanced across at her. "I do, too. I feel that way every time."

Kim shook her head. "Aren't we a serious pair?"

"I still think that's my fault. You want some music? I've got some CDs in the console."

"Let's." Kim opened up the armrest that separated them and took out a couple of plastic cases. "Rod Stewart?"

"Sounds like he's not a favorite," Matt said.

"Not really."

"Those are old standards. 'Moonlight in Vermont.' 'Someone to Watch Over Me.'"

"I didn't know he did songs like that," Kim said. "I

was thinking more 'Wake Up Maggie.'"

"I like these," he said. "It's our parents' music, I suppose."

"I have an album like that. Julie gave it to me. Willie Nelson."

"Good?" Matt asked.

"I love it."

"You want to put one of these in?"

"Why not?" she said. "The two of us can drive down to our kids' house while we listen to our parents' music."

Kim played DJ as they hit the main interstate and cruised east. The ripening Iowa cornfields showed as much yellow as green on their leaves and stalks, and the huge semis swirled the recent dry spell's dust high over the pavement. Normally, Matt would have missed the lush green that had already left the landscape and have had his patience worn thin by the constant parade of trailer trucks. Kim made everything different, playing Rod Stewart and commenting each time a song came on that she really liked. She mixed in Judy Collins next "for some variety" and softly hummed along with "Amazing Grace." She decided to skip the Dan Fogleberg CD because her favorite song on the album "should only be played between Christmas and New Year's." As they put most of Iowa behind them and neared the Mississippi River, an hour and a half had flown by with the same ease that they always shared over coffee.

"Wayne and I come over here every fall," she said. "We like to see the leaves along the river, and there's a restaurant we really like."

"Near here?"

"Right at the next exit."

"What kind of restaurant?"

"Pretty much the standard steaks, chops, chicken, seafood, but really good and a really great view of the river. Wayne likes his steaks."

"Same here, but lately I've sort of been liking fish more."

"I usually get the catfish," Kim said.

"My favorite."

"Really?"

"That and salmon."

"Me, too," she said.

They both laughed.

As the car crested the bluff above the Mississippi, Matt pointed across the river. "Ever been over at that rest stop?"

"Where?"

"On the Illinois side," he said.

"No."

"Beautiful view there, too. You could compare it to the one from Iowa."

"I wouldn't mind a stop," she said.

"Me neither. One stop coming up."

Judy Collins seemed to agree as she sang "Both Sides Now" while they crossed the Mississippi.

CHAPTER EIGHTEEN

A blob of filmy soap bubbles dropped from Matt's wrist as he reached over from the sink for one of the empty glasses on Eric and Julie's kitchen counter. It had been a good day, or the more he thought about it, two great days taking care of little Matt with Kim. In the afternoon, they even had managed a successful expedition downtown with the baby. Matt had forgotten—if he ever knew—how much preparation an outing with a four-month-old required. Kim had checked the diaper bag for supplies, warmed a bottle "just in case," and changed little Matt for a fresh start before they even left the condo. His contribution had been to wedge little Matt's big stroller into big Matt's little car.

Matt put dinner plates in the dishwater and thought that all of the afternoon's elaborate loading and unloading had been worth it. They went downtown to the zoo and gardens in the White River Park. Kim had snugged a tiny baseball cap on little Matt's head to protect him from the sun even though the stroller had a canopy big enough to cover a small patio. Maybe she did it just because it made little Matt look so cute.

They had opted for a walk behind the zoo on a path by the river. The perfectly clear day promised some pretty views. Instead, they found themselves in a canyon formed by huge stone blocks. The wall to the left that enclosed the zoo made sense, but the wall on the other side blocking the view of the river mystified both of them. Luckily, little Matt seemed content with the path as a good place for a stroller ride, and they pushed along with faith that the river would come into view eventually.

As they had walked, the unusual setting continued to puzzle them. Well along the path, they came to a section of stones carved with illustrations and short descriptions of the Empire State Building, the National Cathedral, and the Indiana State Capitol Building. The random appearance of three famous buildings did nothing to clear up their confusion. They finally reached an opening with a glimpse of the river so pedestrian that it gave extra meaning to the term "walking" path. It wasn't until they turned around and retraced their steps that Kim had suddenly said, "Oh, look, Matt." A huge stone block near the start of the path was carved with the story of Indiana limestone and the many famous buildings created from it.

Properly educated, even if in reverse order, they strolled across the wide walking bridge leading toward the heart of downtown. On the other side, young parents pushing their own strollers, joggers in shiny running shorts, guys tossing Frisbees, and a whole cast of summer characters filled the grassy mall that served as the gateway to downtown Indianapolis. It was there that little Matt had decided he didn't care to join the tableau. He fussed a little, and then a little more, and then enough to convince Kim and Matt that they should head back to the condo. Matt had forgotten not only all the preparations it took to get a four-month-old out of the house but also how often such trips ended up being cut short.

He turned his thoughts away from the afternoon and back to dirty dishes. He started to wash the pot from the chicken and noodles in the sink. Kim had done all the cooking on the trip, so he volunteered to clean up. After thirty-two years of marriage, he had forgotten how casual a kitchen could be. Everything felt relaxed with Kim. With no fuss, she made meals that produced leftovers to help out Eric when he returned home alone to take care of little Matt by himself. That meant cooking scalloped potatoes and ham the first night even though she said they weren't "a summer dish." Unlike Carol, she let Matt help peel and cut the potatoes without worrying that every slice was the perfect thickness. The chicken and noodles represented the same strategy of producing leftovers for Eric. It was cute the way Kim mixed, rolled, and cut noodles until flour dusted the kitchen counter, her jeans, her hair, and one of the pastel pullovers she liked to wear.

The noodle-making session had been interrupted by Wayne's daily 8:30 a.m. phone call. He phoned the same time each morning so that he and Kim "wouldn't have to have a full day apart." Matt and Carol had figured talking at home when their respective trips ended would be fine. Wayne, ever the organizer, would have none of that. He called while he and Carol had breakfast in the hotel restaurant so that he could put her on the phone to speak with Matt, as well. Both days, Matt had watched Kim smile and laugh and say "thank you" or "that's a good idea" while Wayne obviously carried the conversation from his end of the line. After a few minutes, Kim would hand Matt the phone, and he would try to say something clever or complimentary or sweet to Carol. It all felt like being on a double date when the other guy was the cool one.

This morning's phone call brought bad news. An elderly deacon at Kim's church had passed away after a long illness. Wayne found the obituary in the online version of the Cedar Rapids newspaper. Now, Kim was taking the time to write a sympathy note while Matt washed the supper dishes. It impressed him that Wayne had been up early reading the morning newspaper on his laptop. It impressed Matt even more that Kim had thought ahead to include a sympathy card when she packed for the trip. Maybe it said as much or more about her kindness than it did about her obvious skill as church secretary. At the moment, she was upstairs searching for the words that would "feel right for Mrs. Kubel."

Kim had given little Matt his bottle as soon as they got home from their afternoon excursion. He went down for a nap and slept right through supper. After eating, Matt and Kim agreed not to use the dishwasher so that the noise wouldn't wake the baby. Matt thought about how nice it would have been to stand at the sink and wash and dry with Kim, but the sympathy card needed her attention. He put the last of the glasses in the cupboard and cleaned up the wet paper towels on the counter just as little Matt's crying from the nursery made the non-dishwasher strategy irrelevant.

"I bet somebody's a little wet," Kim said, poking her head in the kitchen.

Matt hung up the dish towel and figured she meant the baby. He followed her upstairs. He watched as she reached her index finger under the elastic of little Matt's diaper.

"Grandma better take care of this," she said.

She started the process and handed Matt the wet mass of paper and plastic to put in the diaper pail. He watched as she used a wipe and then sprinkled on the baby powder.

"That didn't seem so terrible bad for all of that crying," she cooed. "No, it didn't."

Suddenly little Matt started to squirt again.

Kim covered the stream of pee with her hand. "Matt, some Kleenex, please!"

"Coming right up." He handed her a wad from the tissue box on the changing table.

"That was quite a display," Kim said. A trickle of urine ran down her forearm.

"Looks like he got you," Matt said.

"Just my hand and arm. I think he missed the blouse."

"I think you're right."

"Little boys and their things," she said.

"Did you hear Grandma?" Matt said. "That wasn't a very nice thing to do. You're getting too used to

Grandma waiting on you. Do you think Grandma is a peon? Is that why you peed on Grandma?"

"Oh honestly, Matt." Kim smiled as she gave him a light slap on his hand. "Make yourself useful and get me another one of those wipes."

"Only trying to keep our grandson in line."

Kim glanced at him with the can of baby powder in her hand. "He is our grandson, isn't he?"

"Uh . . . yeah."

"No, think about it, Matt. A part of him is you and a little part of him is me. Think of all those years ago in Ankeny, and now here we are. Here he is. We're both his grandparents."

Matt watched her fasten the tab on the fresh diaper, and everything hit him with the same feeling he could hear in her voice.

"I suppose I'm being foolish," she said.

"No. Not even a little. I know exactly what you're saying. I just don't have the right word for it."

"I think for some things, there aren't words." She paused and looked away. "What do you say we take this little guy in the living room with us?"

"Maybe we can find something on TV. You deserve a little fun after being his servant."

"Also after having him cut our walk short." Kim tickled little Matt under the chin. "You're quite the little tyrant, aren't you?"

They settled into their usual places in the living room: Kim in Julie's chair holding the baby and Matt in Eric's recliner.

"Did you mean that about our walk being cut short?" Matt asked.

"I sort of did."

"Let's go tomorrow," he said.

"Do you think our grandson will have more patience?"

"No, let's make it just the two of us. Julie said they've got a really good sitter. I could call the number."

Kim didn't answer.

"Bad idea, huh?"

"No, I think it's a wonderful idea. I just feel a little guilty. We won't be here that long, and he's such a sweet little guy. He really is, Matt."

"I understand."

Kim wrinkled her nose at the baby and then looked back to Matt. "Let's go anyway. After all, he did just pee on me."

Matt laughed.

Kim lifted up little Matt and nuzzled his neck. "That will teach you to pee on Grandma. Yes, it will, you little stinker. Yes, it will."

Little Matt let out a cute gurgle and drooled on his grandmother's cheek.

CHAPTER NINETEEN

"Here we are," Matt said as he put his car in park. They hadn't made any plans beyond the idea of a late afternoon excursion and an early supper. The zoo and gardens seemed like as good a place as any to start again.

"A little easier without any strollers or car seats to fuss with."

"Agreed," Matt said. He stretched as they got out of the car.

"So why do I miss him already?" Kim asked.

"Because you're a good grandmother. That's what grandmothers do."

"And what do grandfathers do?"

"Try to keep grandmothers happy. What's your pleasure?"

They started to walk in the direction of the ticket and

concession area.

"Have you been to the gardens?" Kim pointed to the entrance.

"No."

"Julie took me. They're beautiful."

"Should we give them a try?"

Kim stopped and looked toward the admission sign at the end of the sidewalk. "I'm not sure. I can't see from here how late they stay open. Plus, they're a little expensive."

"Not a problem," Matt said. "We agreed that tonight would be my treat. It'll make up for all the dates I never took you on in high school."

"Well, the gardens are pretty . . ."

"But?"

"I can't decide. Isn't it terrible to be with a woman who can't make up her mind? Maybe I want to explore."

They started to walk again.

"You've probably been down in the canal area," Matt said. "That's where Eric's office is."

"I haven't."

"Want to take a look?"

"Why not?" Kim said.

"Great. It's an old canal that they redid with sidewalks along the water. It's actually below street level so all the buildings have lower floors that open out on it."

"Sounds interesting."

"It really is," Matt said.

A path between the zoo and gardens led them again to the big pedestrian bridge spanning the river. A conglomeration of people similar to the day before spread out over the bridge and across the grassy mall.

"I thought you'd probably been down to the canal," Matt said.

"We've never come down to Indianapolis very much."

"Same for us."

"That's strange, isn't it," Kim said. "It's not really so far."

"I think it's that way in most families. Your kids grow up, but most of the time, when you get together, it's them coming back home."

Matt stopped beside the concrete bridge railing and pointed toward the football stadium on the edge of downtown. "Eric did take us to a football game one time."

"Julie took us once, too. She got these really good seats because of her job. Wayne was in seventh heaven."

"Our seats were pretty close to heaven." Matt looked skyward. "Way up top! Eric had just moved to town."

"When was that?" Kim asked.

"Four years ago."

"That's when we went, too. What game?"

"Tennessee."

Kim tapped his arm. "You're kidding. That's the one Julie took us to."

"Really?"

"Think of it, Matt. All those years we hadn't seen each other and Julie and Eric hadn't even met then. We were all in that great big stadium at the same time and now they're married, there's little Matt, and here we are."

"Fate?" he asked.

"Something."

"A good something," Matt said. "I'll show you where Eric works."

Though little Matt had stayed home, the mall area had no shortage of SUV strollers. Kim smiled as each baby passed and whispered the occasional "she's a cute one." Matt studied the couples pushing the strollers. Not a single set of grandparents. He wondered what he and Kim had looked like to everybody else yesterday.

"So Eric's office is close?" she asked.

"That cluster of buildings right over there. The canal isn't very wide. Let's take the opposite side. You can see the building better that way."

"This really is something," Kim said as they made their way down a set of stairs. "Look at this. It's all new. It's like its own little world down here."

"It is. I had no idea until Eric showed us. That's his building."

"Very impressive." She looked up and down the canal. "I approve."

"There's something about it," he said. "It's all concrete, but it's still like a little adventure."

Kim stood at attention. "Lead on, sir."

They followed the canal as it made a sharp turn toward the taller buildings in the heart of the city. Up a block, they came to a cast iron fence with a gate that opened into the courtyard of a Native American museum.

"Look, Matt. Look at the garden."

He read the sign on the fence. "Says it's a prairie garden."

"Think we can go in? Do we need a ticket or

something?"

"Let's see."

They wandered toward the museum entrance. Matt couldn't pronounce the name on the building, but it didn't look very Native American to him. He also couldn't tell if they had to pay for the museum to see the garden.

As he stood pondering, Kim glanced back toward the prairie flowers. "It looks like we can just walk through if we want," she said.

"Might as well give it a try."

A winding path snaked through the tall plants. Kim stopped at one with a delicate, round blue flower. She gently brushed the fine petals. "So beautiful."

They walked slowly through the blossoms of white, yellow, lavender, and blue.

"Some of these, we had back when I was a kid in Garwin," he said.

"You had a prairie garden?"

"No, they grew wild. In the ditches or sometimes empty lots. I thought they were just weeds."

"I think they're gorgeous. Imagine when all of Iowa was covered in flowers like this. It must have been unbelievable."

They strolled the entire path as it wound through the garden and back to the gate onto the canal.

"Thank you so much," she said.

"That was fun."

"You are an excellent tour guide."

"I'm afraid I can't take very much credit for something I didn't know anything about."

"You brought us down here."

This time Matt saluted. "Good point. Compliment accepted."

They walked again along the canal looking at offices and condos for sale and an old limestone walking bridge stretching over the water. The only thing they didn't see were any restaurants except for one on the patio of the Indiana Historical Society. When they doubled back, it looked like that building was closing.

"I thought we'd see a place to eat by the canal," Matt said.

"I was having so much fun, I didn't notice."

"I'm thinking we have to go back up to street level."

"I'll trust your judgment," Kim said. "It's been perfect so far."

A flight of stairs took them up to a cavernous street between two huge state office buildings. They walked a block toward the limestone capitol building and its stately dome. At the corner, they paused and glanced in both directions. No restaurants came into sight.

"There's a hotel way down there." Matt pointed in the distance. "It must have a restaurant. Or we could play restaurant roulette."

"Restaurant roulette?"

"Yeah, we walk along and the first restaurant we come to—that's where we eat. A very dangerous game."

Kim smiled. "Why not? I'm feeling adventurous."

"Restaurant roulette it is!"

CHAPTER TWENTY

Restaurant roulette turned out to be a close call. They had only walked three-quarters of a block when a Subway came into view. With no offense to the ubiquitous chain, Matt was happy to see on the corner next to the sub shop a place that billed itself as a neighborhood tavern. Inside, the so-called neighborhood tavern appeared to be an eating and drinking establishment exclusively for young professionals and office workers. Matt had never seen so many people with loosened ties in one location in his life. Of course, young professionals and office workers may have been the only people in the neighborhood. Regardless, the place offered the perfect menu for a light supper. Kim ordered a chicken Caesar salad. He chose the California dream sandwich.

"So," Kim asked "what's in a California dream?"

Matt resisted joking about girls in bikinis. "Grilled chicken with brie cheese, cranberries, pecans, and avocado."

She clucked her tongue. "I don't know. I don't think they grow cranberries in California."

"Okay, but there's the brie. They make lots of cheese in California."

"Sounds French to me."

"Well, you have to give me the avocados," he said. "Definitely lots of avocados in California. I'm pretty sure about the pecans, too."

"We should look up pecans on the internet when we get home. You really ought to know if you've eaten an inauthentic sandwich."

"Okay, we'll fire up the computer as soon as we get back."

Kim fiddled with her napkin. "You think he's doing all right back there?"

"Little Matt?" Big Matt feigned confusion.

"Who else, you goof?"

"I'm sure he's fine. Julie told us the babysitter's very good."

"I know. She said he'd be in good hands if we used the sitter."

"As long as he doesn't pee on those hands."

"That kid." Kim shook her head. "He looked like he was enjoying himself."

"It was a little rude. I'll have to teach him better aim."

"Is that a grandpa job?"

"I don't know," Matt said. "I've never been one before. But, you know, when he gets older, he could go on a camping trip and get in a contest for who's best at putting out the campfire."

"Oh, Matt. I don't know about you." The smile never left her eyes.

"I'm just sayin'."

"Is that what you did when you were a kid?" She rested her chin on her hands and waited for an answer.

"Me, personally? No, but I've heard."

"Right."

"Well, what about girls when they get together?" Matt asked. "What do they do?"

"Certainly not that."

"No, I suppose not."

Kim glanced behind him. "Thank goodness! Rescued by the food."

"Caesar salad," the waitress said. "And one California dream for the gentleman."

Kim nodded toward his plate. "What are those?"

"Sweet potato fries."

"Now that sounds more like Georgia or Alabama than California."

"Eclectic," he said, "maybe that's the theme. California is a very eclectic place."

She took a bite of her salad and seemed to mull over his latest attempt to explain the California dream. "Eclectic. Restaurant roulette. You've always been so smart, Matt."

He laid the sandwich back on his plate. "Uh, possibly not quite smart enough to follow what you're saying."

"Your vocabulary. You've always got the right word for things."

Another evening he might have joked about the

outcome of being married to an English major for thirty-two years. This night, he didn't want thoughts of Carol at the table. "I think you give me too much credit. I don't know how many times I'll be thinking of some word and it's right on the tip of my tongue—"

"And it doesn't come out," Kim said.

"Exactly."

"But everybody does that. I'm thinking about the way you speak in general. It's not like a coach. I mean, I know you are one, but Julie is always interviewing coaches. Sometimes . . . maybe it's mostly the football coaches I'm thinking about. You know what I mean, sometimes they're just so . . ."

"Monosyllabic."

Kim laughed. "See! Vocabulary. The exact thing I was trying to say. I was intimidated by you in high school."

The abrupt shift in the conversation left him at a sudden loss for words. All he could think of was the ache of inadequacy he had felt every time he passed Kim in the hall at Ankeny High.

"I remember you always on the honor roll," she said, "and making National Honor Society."

"You did, too."

"Senior year. Not junior year like you and the other really smart kids."

"Honor Society is Honor Society."

"Well, it's nice of you to say so." She speared some lettuce and a piece of chicken with her fork. "This is really good."

"Mine, too. I like the sweet potato fries. You don't get them everywhere."

"I've never had them. I see them on a menu, but they never sound quite right."

"Here, try." He slid his plate toward her.

"Really?"

"Honest, they're good."

She sampled a small piece. "Mm, you're right."

"Told you."

"Oh, look at that cardinal out there."

Matt glanced toward the window, but didn't see anything. He turned back to see Kim making an elaborate gesture of stealing another fry from his plate.

"See," she said, "Little Matt's not the only one who can be a stinker."

They talked and ate and probably sat too long at the table after declining the waitress' suggestion of coffee. Matt finally put out money for the bill when he noticed the knot of people standing at the hostess station waiting to be seated.

"Thank you," Kim said as they stepped outside.

"I guess we should find our way back to the car."

"It's a beautiful evening for a walk."

"We can take our time," Matt said.

They retraced their steps down to the canal. Kim pointed to the old, arched walking bridge. "Let's go over to the other side."

The narrow steps eased them closer together. Their hands touched, and without a word, their fingers intertwined. A couple on a paddleboat floated beneath the bridge.

"That looks like fun," Matt said.

"This is nice, too." Kim answered softly.

Talking didn't seem important as they walked along

the canal. They passed under a city street above, and an old park at street level came into view.

"Let's go up there," Kim said.

At the top of the stairs, the park spread out around an old bandstand. Antique benches with wooden slats and cast iron frames stood scattered among the oak trees and freshly mown grass. They stopped at a bench with a perfect view down to the prairie garden across the canal.

"Shall we?" Matt nodded at the long bench but hesitated at the choice presented by the cast iron arm in the middle. They could land at separate ends or squeeze close together on one side.

Kim made the decision by staying next to his side as they sat. Matt rested his arm on the back of the bench. The downtown enveloping the park seemed quiet and almost distant in the long silence between them. A lowering orange sun reflected in the glass of the city's tallest skyscraper. In the soft light, they watched small songbirds flit through the tall prairie plants across the canal.

"I never knew Indianapolis was so beautiful," she said softly.

The shadows of the oak trees grew longer with the sinking sun until finally Kim sighed and they both knew it was time to go. Even the thought of little Matt at home didn't make them hurry as they strolled hand-in-hand back toward the zoo, the parking lot, and the ride to Eric and Julie's condo. When they arrived home, they found the sitter reading at the kitchen table with a diet cola at hand.

"Hi, Mr. and Mrs. Cooper," she said.

Neither Kim nor Matt corrected her.

"How was he?" Kim asked.

"You have a very good little boy there. I just now finished giving him a bottle, changing him, and putting him down for the night."

"Thanks very much," Kim said.

Matt paid the sitter who gathered her things and headed out to her car.

As the young woman left, Matt asked Kim, "Should we look in on him?

"Maybe not. He might not quite be asleep. How about later?"

"Makes sense."

"There's a show on I like," she said. "*Castle.*"

"Oh, I love that one. I thought it was on Mondays."

"Summer reruns. It's on at a different time."

"Should we watch?" he asked.

"You might have seen it, already."

"That's okay."

"Good," she said.

They went to the living room and Matt knelt down to turn on the TV and sort through the phalanx of controllers. He turned around to see the sofa empty and Kim seated in Julie's chair. He took his spot back in Eric's recliner.

Matt had watched the show's episode before. Per the series formula, the writer and the lovely detective followed a convoluted set of twists and turns, eventually untangling the crime and not their own relationship.

"That was a good one," Matt said as he clicked off the TV.

"I always like it."

"Think we should go look in on the little guy?"

"Let's."

They walked the stairs single file and found little Matt sleeping with the gentle sounds only babies make. They softly closed the nursery door and stood in front of Kim's room across the hall.

"He seems fine," she said. "I should probably do the night feeding by myself."

"I don't mind getting up with you."

"No, we're heading home tomorrow, and it's a lot of driving for you. You should get your rest."

"You sure?" he asked.

"I think that's best."

He stood in front of her like an uncertain teenager half-afraid to breathe.

"Well, goodnight," she said.

CHAPTER TWENTY-ONE

How do you talk about feelings that don't have a name? Matt hadn't found a way. Part of him was glad when he got hung up at the airport for most of the morning. Eric had taken some kind of red-eye flight out of Mexico City and run into a big delay in Chicago. He called Matt's cell with the new arrival time. Rather than go back to the condo, Matt had decided to wait at the airport.

By the time Eric landed safely and they drove to the condo, Kim had cold cuts, bread, cheese, and fruit on a platter for lunch. The conversation among the three of them started with little Matt and pretty much stayed there. That talk was easy.

The exhausted look on Eric's face told Kim and Matt that they should stay a little longer while he took a nap. He shook his head and told them it was a long way to

Iowa. A call to the babysitter got Eric his relief for the afternoon. By the time the sitter arrived at two o'clock, Matt had a son and a grandson napping in the condo. Kim and Matt took one last look at the baby and then started their trip.

Four-and-a-half hours later, they had almost certainly set a record for how many times two people in a car could remark that the landscape in Illinois was flat. Only an oldies station out of Chicago saved them from the deafening silence of not knowing what to say. They picked up the station in Indianapolis and it carried them almost to Iowa. As the signal started to fade and static punctuated more and more of the songs, Matt turned down the volume.

"Should I look for something else?" he asked.

"If you like. I don't know the stations around here."

"We've had a lot of music. I could turn it off."

"Maybe," she answered.

"It's half past six. You hungry? There's that place across the river you said you liked." He waited for her answer.

"That's kind of Wayne's and my place."

"Right."

"I wish we were on the other side of the highway," she said. "That rest stop we were in on the way out had snack machines. Something like that would be enough for me."

"I can do that."

"It's going the wrong way."

"There's an exit right across the river," he said. "I can double back."

"Do you want to?"

"Sure."

He crossed the bridge and did the loop down the exit, under the highway, and back up the other side.

Kim watched him merge into traffic.

"It's like a carnival ride," he said. He didn't see her smile.

They reached the rest stop ramp and followed a curving access road back to the bluff. He parked and they walked wordlessly to a low building set in among a stand of oaks. Matt stared at the vending machines. The closest thing to an evening entrée was a pack of beef sticks. He could imagine driving the rest of the way to Cedar Rapids with the smell of garlic hanging in the car as heavily as their silence. Women didn't like beef sticks, anyway.

"What looks good?" he asked.

"I don't know."

"Cheese crackers?"

"How about those and cashews," she said.

He reached into his pocket for change. He hadn't noticed the cashews. They seemed like a treat compared to plain old peanuts. "One pack or two?"

"Maybe just one," Kim said.

They each took a can of diet soda and walked to a bench overlooking the river. She spread out some tissues between them and opened the snacks. Her slender fingers broke the cheese crackers into squares and placed them on the makeshift tablecloth. They ate and watched the water flow slowly by in the valley below.

"Was it wrong, Matt?" she suddenly asked. "Was last night so wrong?"

"Maybe not wrong . . . I don't think anybody would

understand."

She flinched and a look of panic filled her eyes.

"I wouldn't tell anybody," he said.

"Oh, no. No. Me either."

"That doesn't mean I think it was wrong."

Kim looked in the direction of a towboat pushing a full load of barges up the river.

Matt studied her profile.

"It's a pretty scene," she said. "You wouldn't think so, would you? Just barges full of coal."

He watched her take a drink of soda and set the can aside. "Do you want to go?" he asked.

"Let's let the sun go down a little more. It won't be so much in your eyes driving."

He leaned back and felt the evening begin to cool. They didn't move until Kim began quietly folding up the tissues on the bench. Matt took her cue and they walked to the car with the sun at their backs and the shadows growing very long like the night before.

He drove two miles and used the first exit to double back toward Iowa. They crossed the river with less than two hours to go. The sun glowed orange and pink and finally an ebony purple.

"It's beautiful," Kim said.

"I'm glad we had this for the end of our trip."

The disappearing light wrapped the car in a blanket of darkness pierced by the headlights of cars and trucks in an unending stream of traffic on the interstate highway.

Kim rested her hand on the storage console between their seats. "I saw you had some classical albums in here."

"A couple," Matt said. "Something to play when I'm not in the mood to sing."

"Do you mind if I play one?"

"That sounds nice."

She picked through the CDs until something caught her fancy. She slipped the disc into the player and Johann Sebastian Bach escorted them across the night-shrouded Iowa prairie. By the time they reached Cedar Rapids, Matt wished that neither the music nor the trip had to end. He guided the car through downtown traffic and back into the quiet of her neighborhood. They drove down the street and saw the lights on in her house.

"Wayne's already home," she said.

"I see. We got a late start."

"Matt, could you pull over?"

He slowed and came to a stop along the curb under a huge maple tree.

"It's been a hard day," she said.

"We didn't talk much."

"No."

"I'm sorry," he said.

"Don't be."

"Okay," he said quietly.

"I just need one thing from you," she said.

Matt waited.

Finally, she turned to him. "Promise me one thing. Promise this trip will always be a good memory."

"I promise," Matt said.

Kim leaned over in the darkened car and kissed him on the cheek.

ABOUT THE AUTHOR

Tom McKay is a historian and museum consultant who lives in his hometown of Hampton, Illinois. His debut novel, *West Fork*, was published by East Hall Press at Augustana College in 2014. His short stories have appeared in the *Wapsipinicon Almanac, Vermont Ink, Downstate Story*, the *Wisconsin River Valley Journal*, the *Book Rack Newsletter*, and the *Out Loud Anthology* series of the Midwest Writing Center.